OUT OF TIME

James sat in his room. Mr. Woodforde's machine was on the desk in front of him. He was scared of it, but he played with it as though it held no particular power. He switched it on and off a few times, watching the needle on the battery indicator rise slowly from zero to nine, and even slightly beyond nine. He drew the machine closer to him, knowing from the burning feeling on his face that he was about to use it again. With sudden carelessness he keyed in random numbers: 45° 25' 15" 45° 25' 15" followed by a date and time: 11:09. 1948, 1400 hours. Then, before he could have second thoughts, trying to ignore the sick feeling in his stomach, he pressed "Enter."

BY JOHN MARSDEN

OUT OF TIME

JOHN MARSDEN

TOR® A TOM DOHERTY ASSOCIATES BOOK   NEW YORK

This is a work of fiction. All of the characters, organizations, and events portrayed in this novel are either products of the author's imagination or are used fictitiously.

OUT OF TIME

Copyright © 1990 by John Marsden

Originally published by Pan Books, an imprint of Pan Macmillan Australia Pty, Ltd., in Sydney, Australia, in 1990.

A Tor Book
Published by Tom Doherty Associates, LLC
175 Fifth Avenue
New York, NY 10010

www.tor.com

Tor® is a registered trademark of Tom Doherty Associates, LLC.

ISBN-13: 978-0-765-35303-0
ISBN-10: 0-765-35303-2

First Tor Teen Edition: May 2007

Printed in the United States of America

0 9 8 7 6 5 4 3 2 1

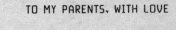
TO MY PARENTS, WITH LOVE

ACKNOWLEDGMENTS

Thanks to Mrs. Thora Dearnley for her typing and patient re-typing.
Also to Natalie Deans, Poss Herbert, and Justin Lee for stories.

And special thanks to Penny Hueston, Roxarne Burns, and James
Fraser at Pan.

OUT OF TIME

B ROWSING THROUGH *The Book of Lists* late one night, James read this paragraph, as he pulled at his bottom lip with an anxious finger:

> "On July 6, 1944, the Ringling Brothers and Barnum & Bailey circus was giving a performance in Hartford, Conn., before 7,000 paid [sic] customers. A fire broke out: 168 persons died in the blaze and 487 were injured. One of the dead, a small girl, thought to be six years old, was unidentified. Since no one came to claim her and since her face was unmarred, a photograph was taken of her and distributed locally, and then throughout the U.S. Days passed, weeks and months passed, but no relative, no playmate, no one in the nation came forward to identify her. She remains unknown to this day."

James put the book down and gazed out of his open bedroom window. It was dark outside, a kind of molten dark that slid endlessly through the window. James sat at the edge of the island of light created by his desk lamp. He turned the light off and let the black fill the room. It was a warm night. The screen that had been on the window sat propped against the wall where it had rested for two months, discarded and dusty.

There was a huge tree outside the window. It blocked much of the view but was itself a view. Old and oak, it was a treasury of hollow places. In its dark green curves dwelt old air, unbreathed pockets. Possums ran along the branch that led right to James' window. When not fighting or mating they fed from his long friendly fingers.

It seemed that the tree itself was reaching into the room: if the windows were closed it brushed and scratched against them. When the windows were open it became a living curtain of green. The boy was not sure whether the tree was friendly or not. On the whole he thought he liked it, but sometimes when he was in bed and the lights were out, it scared him with its incessant rubbing on the glass.

The soft sweet dark air flooded around James. He was no longer sure where his room ended and the night began. Across the square in one of the old laboratories a light came on. Directly above it a thin rind of crescent moon showed pale in the sky; pale compared to the solid artificial light in the distant lab. "Artificial light," James wondered, "what does that mean, 'artificial?'" He held out his hands to the darkness and let it wash between his fingers. Then, possumlike, he swung out across the windowsill onto the nearest branch of the oak, crawled along it and squeezed down the trunk to the ground. Behind him the house still squatted.

James ran around the edges of the square, like the last line of a wave on a beach, that is, in shallow curves and fretting lines. Nowhere did he take the shortest distance between two points.

He merged with shadows and slipped easily through the cool patches under the trees. The big brick lab, Building H, two dull stories high, opaque and severe, kept its blind eyes closed as he swerved past it. He was running toward the light. The light came from an old weatherboard building at the center of a cluster of small storage sheds and garages. It was, as James knew, Lab 17, the smallest of the network of old laboratories. The night was warm, and so the door, defying the regulations, was half-open. James, head down, with the overconfidence born of familiarity, came sliding in as if on a skateboard. He tumble-turned against the first workbench and ran into a corner, hiding between two globes of the world, one old, one new. From there he peered at the man working at the front bench.

Mr. Woodforde at first glance looked more like an accountant than a physicist. A man of about seventy, he was completely bald and dressed in a neat dark pinstripe suit. He was small and wrinkled and had a mouth full of gold-capped teeth. His skin had the grayish color of a heavy smoker. His eyes hung like fried eggs, in bags of age.

At James' entrance he looked up briefly, then returned to his work. He wrote down a series of numbers before speaking. His voice was surprisingly rounded and rich and resonant.

"How fortunate that I wasn't delicately balancing a vial of sulfuric acid above a tray of water," he remarked. James smirked from between the two globes. He liked the formal way Mr. Woodforde spoke. For the next few minutes there was a silence in the lab: only the little sounds of pen on paper, the door whining with an occasional movement of air, trees giving a shrug of leaves outside the windows. James emerged from his shelter shyly, by degrees. He doodled with his finger along a side bench,

13

traced an oblique path toward the blackboard at the front of the lab, followed his own course there. He took a piece of chalk and wrote on the blackboard: "MY NAME IS JAMES, ABSOLUTELY." Then he wriggled around the front sink to where Mr. Woodforde was standing, and stood behind him, looking around his elbow at the papers and equipment spread across the table. Mr. Woodforde showed no awareness of his presence, except to mutter:

"Look on, you enforcers of the Official Secrets Act, and despair."

He continued to work in silence on a small circuit board, until, his eyes tired, he nudged it away and put down his pliers.

"I can't believe it's going to work. Everything tells me it's going to work, except for my instincts. With everything else I've achieved it's been the other way round." He sighed and turned to James, who gazed impassively into his face. "You know, James," he said, "revenge is a wonderful motive. If they hadn't rushed me in here to make room for all the fancy Americans, I would have happily eked out my time doing research on superconductors. Now, there they are in their brand-new maximum-security fortress, working out how to detect low-flying mosquitoes, while the forgotten old man works in a shed out the back winning a Nobel Prize. And the second greatest satisfaction I'll get out of all this is to be able to clench my fist and render my radius and ulna perpendicular to my humerus." He chuckled and interpreted: "Bend my arm at the elbow." Then he added thoughtfully, "I know the greatest satisfaction will be to . . . well, I'll use the cliché . . . 'go where no man has gone before.' But there's a failure of my imagination somewhere. Maybe that's why I don't really think it'll work. I can't imagine it." He glanced again at the boy, who was watching him with respect. "I've said too much again. But who knows how much of it you absorb? And I don't think you're likely to be suborned by foreign agents. You've got the perfect defense. Funny," he mused, "I hadn't thought about this being used for defense purposes, but no doubt someone will think of an application." He sighed and turned back to his work. "No sleep, no food, no exercise. I can't run on adrenalin all the time."

JAMES SAT in class with books spread around him. A mosaic of books, each one open, each with its story to tell. James swam in the colors and words, swam deep, emerging only once to glance shyly around the room. Bright parrots startled across one page onto another, snakes tumbled out of there to writhe in an ecstasy of confusion among the silent pyramids, sand blew through the Andes into the eyes of flat-faced knights on over-developed horses. James traced a journey through them all, a route that ignored time and borders and politics. He dipped his hand into history as he wandered among geography.

One of the biggest books at his table was called *Minter's Illustrated Atlas of the World and All It Contains*. James had not seen it before and was not surprised to find, when he opened it, an inscription at the front stating: "A Gift to the Library from Daniel Woodforde." As he scanned its brightly colored pages a name on a map caught his eye. It was a map of the state of Connecticut, in the U.S. The name swam in his mind. Gradually the colors of the map gave way to a charcoal vision. James saw an army of lost people marching out of the book: a little girl came from Connecticut to join a line of Incas and conquistadors from

Peru; they in turn met up with nameless bloated bodies rising out of the sea, mad World War II survivors from Pacific islands, and desperate beaten millions of Kampucheans. From Melbourne came a shy dark man in the clothing of 1942. From Russia came thousands of soldiers—illiterate peasants who, conscripted in World War II and later discharged, ignorant of the name or location of their own villages, spent the rest of their lives wandering Russian roads in search of their homes. And from all over the world came the saddest figures in history, the Unknown Soldiers of every country, the unidentified men and women, the brave and the frightened, the pale and the lost.

James quailed before the crowds. He understood in some part of his being how much they wanted to be recognized. But he knew they wanted even more. Perhaps he understood how inseparable their needs were. But the numbers panicked him. He could think only of one at a time. He slammed the book shut and left the room.

IT WAS three o'clock in the afternoon in Mr. Woodforde's Lab 17. Strips of dusty sunlight stretched across the books and tables. The light husks of dead insects lay still on the window. Mr. Woodforde was perched on a high stool, a jeweler's glass screwed into his eye as he worked on some electronic circuitry. James was playing with a cobweb at the end of the same bench. He strummed it lightly with a finger, watching its spider hang on grimly, hunched into a corner of the web.

"Damn!" Mr. Woodforde said. James left the web and came to him. He sat on the opposite side of the bench, watching with interest. Mr. Woodforde leaned back, took the glass out of his eye and rubbed his face with tired fingers. Then he laughed delightedly.

"Pretty close," he said. "Pretty close. And the closer I get, the prettier it is." James slid across the bench for a better view. He thought at first that he was looking at nothing more than a mathematical calculator. Mr. Woodforde had assembled all the pieces into a black case that resembled either a calculator or a remote control for a television. There were four panels of buttons, two aerials, and a screen, but they were all on a small enough scale to be fitted into a hand-sized case.

"I'm just working on mechanical details now," Mr. Woodforde explained. "Design trivia." He muttered to himself, almost humming it as a tune: "Latitude on the top line, longitude on the second, date on the third, time on the fourth. Or date up the top? Doesn't really matter." He stood looking out the window for a minute. "In an emergency what you'd need is a return key. Put your home coordinates in the memory, along with the time. That's easy. Could save a life. Could be my life that's saved." He looked up at the blackboard and James followed his glance. Written there was a series of numbers: 150° 50' 51", 34° 15' 21".

"Very important numbers, James," Mr. Woodforde commented. "They tell you where you are. These numbers pin us to this spot, as surely as a butterfly that's stuck on a board with a thumbtack. Doesn't matter where you're located on the surface of this earth, a series of half a dozen numbers can put you within a block of home. I tell you what, those numbers are carved into my memory forward, backward, and inside out. If I find myself in the middle of a battle in the Dardanelles in 1915, I may well be keen to get home in a hurry. But I like the idea of a return key."

In the distance a church bell rang. James pushed himself up from the bench and stretched onto the floor. He began a circuitous route toward the door. Mr. Woodforde was doing calculations on the blackboard, ignoring him. But as the boy reached the door the man called out:

"Oh here. I nearly forgot. Got a book for you. Thought you might like it. I've finished with it." He threw it to James, who darted and caught it then ran out of the lab, looking at the book's title as he went.

It was called *The Time Machine* by H.G. Wells.

THE SCHOOL teemed with life. James was reminded of a film he had seen in Science, a film of maggots consuming the corpse of a sheep. The film had been speeded up: two or three days compressed into ten minutes. The effect had been startling. The maggots swarmed with energy, a frantic mass. In ten minutes they reduced the sheep's body to a forlorn skeleton, white bones sticking up like tree branches in winter, like a school at weekends.

It was the 12:30 bell that had spilled the school into this froth of movement. Bare playgrounds and empty corridors streamed with people. Their voices bubbled and foamed. In their wake came James, books held to his chest, gliding down the corridor like a canoeist. Most of the crowd turned left, onto the bitumen playground, but James turned right, into the library. Without looking up or around he crossed the carpet to a corner near the heater. He nestled down on the floor and glanced along the nearest shelf. It was the H section. Hardy: *Jude the Obscure*; Hare; Harker; Harnett; Harris; Harrison: *Legends of the Fall*.

The title intrigued him. He took it out and flicked through it, but it looked too difficult. He put it back and continued his perusal. Haser, Hastings, Hautzig, Hawthorne, Hayes, Hazzard. He ran his finger down the spine of *The Endless Steppe,* but he had read it twice already.

A little frustrated he went back up a shelf and found Guest: *Ordinary People.* He had heard older kids talking about this book. He took it down, opened it, spent a few moments flirting with the cover, the title page, the acknowledgments, and then with a deep sigh of satisfaction, began reading the first paragraph.

THE HOME run by the Sisters of Mercy was at the end of a lane in the backyard of the town, a place of dumped cars and old shacks and abandoned projects. The river ran close by; the same river that in other places moved with slow dignity but here dribbled contemptuously past, an ooze of gray soapy water. Despite the nuns' occasional tired admonitions the kids played near it, by it, in it. A few had been drowned over the years; no one could remember how many.

The orphanage had a name, though not many noticed it or remembered it: the Maria Torreon Home. It had been endowed by an Army general who had lost his wife years before, and still dolefully mourned for her.

Most of the nuns were Mexican, though there were a few outsiders—Nicaraguans mostly, and an Italian-English nun named Sister Agnes, who had been there forever. Occasionally someone from North America would come for a short term on an exchange program, while one of the Mexican sisters went to

Los Angeles to take her place. The only member of the community to look forward to these exchanges was the one going to California.

Sister Josephine from the Hospice of the Sacred Heart in Oakland, California, had been at the orphanage several days before the children began to take on individual form for her. Until then they had been a confusion of black-haired dark-skinned bodies, some quick and darting, some ponderous and heavy.

Not surprisingly, one of the first children to become a recognizable being for her was the only child in the orphanage of Anglo-Saxon appearance. A boy of about ten, he had the blond hair and lightly tanned skin of the young nun's little brother at home in the States. Yet this boy was different. He had a disconcerting way of looking through people. He looked right into their eyes but appeared to see nothing. He did not respond to the friendly greetings Sister Josephine began to offer whenever their paths crossed, and some instinct told her not to press for an answer. At the first opportunity, however, she started asking other nuns about the boy. The answers were hardly satisfactory. He was named Grigor; he had been plucked off the streets where he had been living the usual life of a child-beggar; he kept to himself, communicating with no one; he "could be" North American, but was more likely to be half-caste; he was obsessed with airplanes.

Sister Josephine had the opportunity herself to witness this last idiosyncracy. Whenever the small silver wedge of an airplane appeared in the sky, Grigor became agitated and excited, pointing to it and jumping up and down. It was hard to tell what emotion he was expressing, as the sounds he emitted belonged to no recognizable language. Grigor spent much of his time drawing in the dirt; when the American nun knelt beside him one day to look at his drawings, she realized that they were all drawings of aircraft. She supplied him with paper and a pencil and watched, curious, as he transferred his dirt drawings to the paper. Something that had not been clear in the dust of the Mexican orphanage became apparent on the new surface: his airplanes were all shown in a wrecked state. They were all crashed upon the ground, with bodies strewn around them.

As she watched Grigor, a terrible theory began to form in Sister Josephine's mind. Supposing this was an American boy? Supposing he had been in a plane crash, surviving where others had not? Supposing he had wandered away from the wreckage before the rescuers came, so that he was presumed to have died along with his fellow travelers? And, too young and too shocked to explain his predicament, had ended up in the streets, struggling to stay alive? The scenario was plausible; it did not require a leap of the imagination, just a few hops.

The young nun put her theory to her supervisor. Sister Angelique heard her through, her only expression a little smile. The smile grew as the American talked, but never became mocking.

"You Americans," she said at last, "you are so romantic."

"But," Sister Josephine argued, "it is possible."

"Oh yes, it is possible."

"Would you mind if I tried to find out a little more?"

Sister Angelique considered for a long time.

"You may do so," she at last conceded, "as long as the child's stability is not affected. And as long as you do not become distracted from your other duties. There is only room for one obsession in the Church."

Armed with this license, Josephine began her search for Grigor's past. She conducted it with as much energy as she could muster in the slow humidity of Mexico. But her energy was not matched by anyone else whom she tried to enlist. Her efforts were met with indifference or amusement. "Crazy gringo" seemed to be the unspoken attitude. "One street kid, what does it matter? American, Mexican, Eskimo, who cares?" No one seemed to have a particular memory of Grigor, nor of his antecedents.

In desperation, as her stay in Mexico drew to a close, the sister visited the U.S. Consulate and explained the case to the Consul. The Consul listened indulgently, then threw back her head and laughed. "Well," she said, "That's a new one! They didn't brief us on that at the State Department! But you must forgive me if I say that your story, though wonderfully seductive, is a bit thin. And too far-fetched for the Diplomatic Corps!" But she was curious enough to come out to the Maria Torreon Home to visit Grigor, who was as indifferent to her as he was to everyone else. "Surely," the Consul asked, "if he was American, he would respond more enthusiastically to you and me?" Sister Josephine was forced to agree that this was a weakness in her case.

On her last day the nun bought a present for the perplexing little boy. She chose the obvious gift, one that was sure to delight, a model of a jet, painted white with a red stripe. As she walked to the car that was waiting to take her to the airport she detoured to give the model to the child. He saw it in her hand, stared, grabbed at it. Then he said, in urgent, perfect English: "Fasten your safety belts. Put your head between your knees." He ran away, through the dust, across the yard, away from the astonished face of the young Californian sister.

JAMES CAME up the steps after school, zigzagging from side to side and missing every third step. The cockatoo's cage was swinging on the verandah, as though it had been given a push by a passerby. A leaf dropping lazily from an elm tree reached something—a gap in the air?—and skidded downward in a quick and sudden spiral. James slipped around it and continued along the verandah, to enter the house by a side door.

He visited the kitchen before going upstairs to his room. The woman there turned around when he came in.

"Oh, James," she said. "Do you want a sandwich? I've made myself a late lunch."

James waited for his sandwich, then took it, on its plate, along with a glass of milk and his schoolbag, upstairs: a journey that was a triumph of balance and coordination. He ate the sandwich at his desk, watching the oak tree with practiced eyes. Its green was too green, its brown too brown for him to believe in it, but he liked its daytime softness and color, so different from the silver and gray of night.

A fragment of music drifted up the stairs and slipped into the room like steam. James cocked his head, mouth open, the half-eaten sandwich stuck in the air.

"Coming to the signpost," the husky voice on the tape sang,

> "Coming to the signpost
> I can't look where I'm going to,
> I can't see where I'm going,
> Till I first see where I've been."

The tape was abruptly turned off, there was a clatter of laughter, loud voices, and footsteps. A door slammed. James reached out over the windowsill, almost past his center of balance, and touched the branch of the tree. He ran his warm hand along it, prodding at the little bumps and buds. The surface looked rough but felt smooth. Through the crowds of leaves he could see people moving across the square: tiny snapshots of black or pinkish-white skin, a cap, a mustache, a pair of boots, a smiling mouth, a Security badge on a gray-green lapel. Framed in the widest gap was the portico and door of the main Administration building. As James scanned the square, the door of the big white building opened, and the Director came out. He paused on the top step for a moment, and stood glancing around him. James became very still. The Director, perfectly groomed, trim in his light-gray suit, nodded as one of the Americans passed him, then continued his perusal of the quadrangle. Suddenly his face tilted up a little until he seemed to be looking right at James' window. James stood back in the shadows, his mouth slightly open, not daring to move. After a moment the Director's mood changed: as though a button had been pressed he set off briskly toward the new lab, Building H. But for some minutes after he had gone from sight, James still stood aside, the shadows of the leaves dappling his body.

JAMES SLIPPED silently into Mr. Woodforde's lab. A meter inside the door he braked, waiting, then tiptoed forward. Mr. Woodforde, old and tired and overdone, was asleep, head down on the front desk, glasses slanting across his nose. James stopped again and watched. Then something about the stillness of the man caused him to wait on his breath, to open his mouth, and prickle all over. Nothing moved in the lab, not the fly on the window, not the electric fan overhead, not the eyes or mouth or chest of the still man. His stillness was not sleep. His stillness was suddenly reflected in James, who himself went into a kind of death, that lasted . . . how long? Perhaps only two or three minutes.

James moved forward, directly for once, his usual wanderings cut off by the power of death. He did not touch Mr. Woodforde, but stared at him closely, his face just centimeters away from the man's. There was a kind of dullness about the skin that he intensely disliked. He looked away, along the bench. He saw the familiar notebooks, a couple of calculators, a pile of books, and there, in the middle of it all, surrounded by pens and tools and pieces of chalk, the calculator-sized piece of equipment that Mr. Woodforde had been making.

James picked it up. It looked finished. He examined it closely. He had a good understanding of what Mr. Woodforde had been building and of what the scientist had believed this machine could do. It never occurred to James to doubt the concept but he did not know whether his friend had completed the task. He turned it over curiously in his hand. It looked complex, but robust. He inspected it closely. Each of the four panels contained all the numbers from 0 to 9. James set himself to remember some details. Top panel, latitude; second, longitude; third, date; and fourth, time. Or was it time, then date? James carefully pressed in the coordinates that Mr. Woodforde had written on the blackboard that day: 150° 50' 51", 34° 15' 21". Then he keyed in the date. He didn't know whether to put the 19 in front of the year so he left it out. Then, with a pale sidelong glance at Mr. Woodforde's body, he keyed in 3:44, not the correct time, but two minutes earlier.

There were two more keys at the bottom, one marked "Enter" and the other "Return." Greatly daring, James pressed "Enter." There was a pause. Then the little screen flashed up the words: INSUFFICIENT INTEGERS ENTERED.

James was now in a quandary. He thought the message on the screen might refer to the missing prefix of 19, but he wasn't sure what integers were. He also didn't like being in the lab with a dead body. He had loved Mr. Woodforde but he hated his body. And finally, although he had never heard of anyone but himself and occasional cleaners visiting Lab 17, he did not want to risk being caught there. He had already made up his mind to take the machine with him; if he was caught in the room the opportunity would be lost.

He squeezed the machine into his pocket, grabbed a few pieces of paper that Mr. Woodforde had been writing on, and sidled around the room to the door. Without a backward glance he left the lab and ran counterclockwise around the square. He reached his bedroom by shinnying up the oak tree and crawling precariously along the branch. At last, sitting at his desk, panting with fear and excitement and tiredness, he pulled out the papers from Mr. Woodforde's workbench.

He was hoping to find instructions for the use of the machine on the sheets. Nervously he started reading:

The work of Roy P. Kerr (1963) on the structures of black holes, and the contributions of Martin Kruskal of Princeton on the consequences of the black hole/white hole relationship, led to the hypothesis that Wheeler and Faynman's single particle theory and Kruskal's theory of a parallel universe were the key to escaping from the linear sequential model of time. It was further hypothesized that an extraordinary energy source, enabling the subject to jump through the ring singularity of the rotating black hole, would enable the subject to pass at will between the parallel universes.

Work commenced in December 2004 at the National Defense Forces' Research Center, with the first object of discovering or developing a means to facilitate travel faster than light and hence to control the transfer of matter to antimatter. I can now state that such a means has been devised, which has passed all tests and opened remarkable possibilities to physicists as well as members of other disciplines.

There was much more of this, punctuated by comments in the margin by Mr. Woodforde that seemed to be little jokes he was making with himself, like "pause for gasps of wonder" next to the second paragraph and "beware of overkill." James read the margin comments and the first two paragraphs of the text, but even those he did not understand. The article stopped abruptly, apparently in the middle of a paragraph, on the fourth page.

James sighed, put the notes aside, and picked up the machine. It did not look like a machine but he did not know what else to call it. He started to press in numbers again, and although he kept doing so until he was too tired to continue, he had no success. Nothing seemed to happen.

IN THE morning while James was passing the window to reach his wardrobe, he became dimly aware of a faint clamor across the square. He stopped and looked out. The sight was, to him, unprecedented. People were coming in and out of Lab 17. As he watched, two Security officers came out of the lab and walked toward the main Administration building. On their way they passed a woman in a white coat, someone whom James hadn't seen before. A few minutes later, a gray station wagon backed in near the lab.

James' first instinct was to rush into his clothes and leave the house to insinuate himself in whatever was happening. But his second thoughts were wiser. He realized that he had to keep away from Lab 17. Any appearance he made there now might cause someone to make connections. The sight of him in the area might trigger off a series of speculations: "He's been around here a few times, hasn't he? . . . I think he even went into the lab occasionally . . . Woodforde was pretty good with him, didn't mind him hanging around . . . wonder if he's been in there since Woodforde died? Shouldn't there have been more of Woodforde's work in that lab? . . . Grab that kid for a sec, ask him a few questions. He understands what you say to him well enough . . ."

James stayed where he was. He kept watching. Nothing much happened for quite a time. Just before lunch, a stretcher with a covered-body shape on it was carried out and loaded into the station wagon. A few passersby glanced at it with curiosity but kept walking. The station wagon drove away.

James went downstairs to get some lunch, then returned to his room, stuffed the device in his pocket, and left the house. He went to the entrance of the complex, passed through the security barriers, went past the big white sign saying "Between 1800 and 0900 all vehicles must use Gate 3," and through the line of pine trees into the Toyne Paddock.

It was not an attractive paddock. It was on the road to the tip, so plastic bags and sheets of newspaper were always scattered across it, flitting toward other destinations. The field was bare and clodded, with scruffy patches of grass. James squatted near the middle of the field, behind a mound of earth that provided a windbreak. With some difficulty he extricated the machine from his pocket and sat looking at it. He had tried, he thought, every possible variation, with no result. Perhaps after all Mr. Woodforde had been old and stupid and had been wrong about the whole thing.

A large piece of paper blew toward him, almost into his face. Suddenly James' mind cleared. He remembered the sign at the entrance to the Center. "Between 1800 and 0900 . . ." Wasn't it likely that Mr. Woodforde would use military time? Feverishly he started pushing numbers into the calculator . . . 150° 50' 51", 34° 15' 21" . . . Again he paused at the date, finally resolving on the compromise of a zero in front of the month, but no century in front of the year. And then the time, going back four minutes, and pressing 1327. And, with mouth as dry as corn chips, he pressed "Enter."

Still nothing. He started again, undeterred, confident. 150° 50' 51", 34° 15' 21", and this time the date with the century prefix. The time, 1328. Enter.

Suddenly, for the briefest instant of time, for a blink, James saw nothing. Not a blankness, not a grayness or blackness, not a wall, not a vast open space, but nothing. He felt disgustingly sick in the stomach. Then, at enormous speed, waves of dizziness pulsated through his body, as though he was being rocked by all the storms in all the ships in all the seas of the world. He realized he had shut his eyes at some stage and that they were still shut, but that was the only coherent thought he had. He had no inclination to open them, did not even think of it, could not form intentions. He felt that he was coming apart, ceasing to be. Until, with equally dazzling sudden speed, he felt his body tingling together again, stinging into a kind of giddy, staggering unity. He was on his feet, lurching a little, then stable, settled, with nothing worse than a ringing in his ears. His legs started to move, his senses to operate. He was just a few steps from the mound in the middle of the paddock. He went to it and squatted behind it, then extricated the machine from his pocket and looked at it. A large sheet of newspaper blew toward him, almost into his face. Suddenly he was filled with a tearing panic. Gritting his teeth he pressed "Return" on the machine. Again there was the shocking glimpse of nothing before the disgusting sickness rocked through him, and the dizziness, the fuzziness, the sense that he had become empty inside and out.

And there he was, standing on a street corner. He looked blankly around him, failing to recognize the scene. It took several seconds before he slowly identified it as the corner of Handbury Road and Wilson Street, about two blocks from the Center, about three blocks from the Toyne Paddock. He looked at his watch. It said 1:33. He assumed that he was back in the present. Then he realized that he would never know.

MOST OF that afternoon James wandered restlessly around his room, picking the machine up and fingering it, putting it down again. He felt confused and shaky, and he thought he had a headache. Several times he felt an overwhelming desire to go and hang around Mr. Woodforde's lab, and twice he actually started getting out the window to go there. It was only then that this death, the death of his friend, began to have meaning for him. He realized that it meant "never again," it meant "an end," it meant changes forced upon him. Now when he swung a leg out of the window he might as well swing it right back in. Once again, a slice of his life had been cut out: it had not been replaced and in its stead was nothing. Eventually some sand might dribble in and occupy the same space, but sand was always and only sand.

Halfway through the afternoon he lay on his bed and cried a little into his pillow. His thoughts were for himself; his misery was his own. He did not know that his tears were the only tears shed by anyone as a result of Mr. Woodforde's death.

Later, as he hung out of his window, he heard two Americans talking in the square below.

". . . yeah, I heard some guy hit the eject button, out in one of the old laboratories."

"Yeah, Woodfull, some name like that. Big star once, according to Gary. Child prodigy, you know? Could spell 'physics' when he was six years old."

"Hell, I still can't spell it. So what was he doing out there? Was he working on anything?"

"Just playing around, I think. They let him have one of the

old labs, out of respect. Gary said there was nothing in there, just books, and piles of papers, calculations. But the numbers didn't add up to anything."

"I heard he was dead three days before they found him."

"Not three days. A day and a half maybe. Yeah, pretty sad. That's how we'll all end up."

They walked across to the canteen, unconscious of the boy in the leaves above them. James, precisely and sharply, peeled a leaf from a twig and sat, twirling it in his fingers. Then he dropped it and watched it fall, spinning, knocked into new alignments by branches and air pockets and other leaves. At last it landed on the ground where it lay still and lifeless. A moment later a Security officer walking to Building H crushed it under his unfeeling boot.

A LONG time ago their parents had gone out. James wasn't sure where, but he remembered them saying, "Be good kids, we won't be long." James was too absorbed in a game he was playing with a long thin string of ants to take much notice. He was trying to build a zigzag highway for the ants, trying to train them to take a new route.

While he was doing that, Ellie was giving her parents a nice surprise by cleaning the house. At the age of three, her idea of cleaning the house quickly and efficiently was to drag the garden hose in, turn on the tap, and wash down all the furniture.

She'd been at it some time when their parents came home, so the house was pretty waterlogged. They'd had to throw a lot of stuff out. The carpet had grown moldy and the budgie, which had been soaked, got pneumonia and died. It had been a long time before things were back to normal. The funny thing was that James had gotten in more trouble than Ellie. That didn't seem fair to him. He'd never been able to figure it out.

And there were other times, too. Like in Grade Four when he had a teacher called Mrs. Kittenmaster, who at home he always referred to as Kitty, or Pussy. When Ellie came to the school fete James took her to meet Mrs. Kittenmaster. He said to Mrs. Kittenmaster, proudly, "This is my sister, Ellie," and to Ellie he said, "This is my teacher," and Ellie shyly, innocently whispered, "Hello Mrs. Pussy."

It had been a while before he could laugh about that one.

She was a good kid though. He'd been sick with scarlet fever and she'd been terribly upset, hanging round his room all the time and sending in her Teddies and cooking things for him and lending him everything she could think of. She was OK.

THE TELEVISION news was coming to an end. James sat on his windowsill, languidly watching the small set on the white cupboard. The sports news was over, and the sharp-looking man who read the main stories filled the screen again. "This week," he was saying, "is Missing Persons' Week. All week we'll be featuring case histories supplied to us by the Missing Persons Bureau and the Red Cross. If you have any information about these people, or anyone else whom you know to be on Police files, we'll be giving you a number to call. In many of these cases, grave fears are held for the person's safety.

"This morning we have Carla Robinson." A photograph of an attractive smiling teenager appeared. The newsreader's voice went on: "Carla disappeared twenty months ago on August 2nd at 3:50 P.M. near her home in Krogmann. She was thirteen years old. Carla was last seen waiting to cross the road at Krogmann Post Office. She was on her way to post some letters for her mother. The letters were never posted, and neither Carla nor the letters have been seen since. Police believe she may still be alive, but have no clue as to her present whereabouts. If you can help, please ring 008 42 3444. You need not give your name, and all information will be treated as confidential."

James was hunched forward, watching the set. His hands were clasped around his knees and his mouth was open. It was several minutes after the program ended before he broke his concentration. Then he got up and went to his desk, where he added the name "Carla Robinson" to a list on the wall. The name immediately above Carla's was that of Benjamin S. Briggs. There was a note beside his name: 38° 20' 15", 17° 15' 25", December 5, 1972, 3 P.M.

Picking up his schoolbag James went swiftly out of his room and down the stairs in a mathematical progression, jumping first one step, then two, then three, and finally four, with a resounding leap. The front door was open but he went out the side door instead. He leaped off the verandah, steered a course in and out of a series of shrubs, then squeezed through a gap in the fence. The Director was walking decisively across the square, face set toward the Computer Center. He did not see James but James saw him. He crouched behind a tree until the Director was gone, then continued on his meandering journey toward school.

When he arrived in class, lessons had already started. He slipped into the room and sat in a corner, half-obscured by a filing cabinet and a potted plant. The students were engaged in discussion of a novel they had been studying, *Displaced Person*.

The first question James heard asked by the teacher was, "Why does Graeme have a poster of Mars, the surface of Mars, on his bedroom wall?"

"Because the world he's living in is equally gray and bare," James thought.

A hand went up and a girl answered, "Because it's as alien as the world that he's living in."

"Yes, that's right," the teacher agreed. "And what about the movie, *Beauty and the Beast*? Why does the author have Graeme going to a cinema to see that?"

"Graeme is like the Beast," James thought. "For a time, he becomes a beast himself." As he was thinking that, a boy on the other side of the room was explaining, "Graeme goes through a time where he knows what it's like to be a beast. He's a sort of beast in the modern world."

James idly plucked a leaf from the potted plant. The plant was about a meter tall, with shiny green leaves that looked artificial. He flicked the leaf at the soil from which the plant grew. Then he stripped off another leaf, and planted it in the soil, stalk first, so it stood there like a tiny green notice board. He planted another leaf beside it, then scattered a few more randomly around the base of the plant. Within a few moments, rather to his surprise, he realized he had come to the last leaf. With only a flicker of hesitation he removed it too and dropped it on the floor. The plant stood, bare and ugly. Was it still alive? James did not know. It looked like an oil rig, or a rocket launching tower. James had thought that by stripping away its leaves he would reveal its secrets. But it had no secrets. Under all its coverings it was just an old stick. The leaves were part of the plant, not just a covering. In stripping its protection to reveal its mystery, he had stripped away its mystery. The implications of this shocked him. He turned away.

"James! Oh, James. How could you do that? What have you done?" The teacher was swelling in size as she came toward him. "Oh, you're hopeless. Get away from there. Marie! Marie!"

The teacher's aide hurried across the room, "Sorry, Mrs. Chalmers. I was checking Errol's homework."

"Take him over to the language lab. He can listen to a tape. Oh, my poor plant. It just makes you want to give up."

TO GET back from school James tried to take a new route each day. If he could not go by different streets he at least varied the way he walked, or the place where he crossed the road, or the side of the street he used. But as the months passed it became harder and harder to make meaningful changes. So he was delighted one afternoon when he noticed that the gates to the football oval were unlocked. This meant he could take a short cut to Wilson Street. He walked through the gates and entered a narrow gap between two grandstands. He emerged into the sun again and clambered across a low fence on to the playing area.

There were about ten boys kicking a football but they were far enough away for James to ignore them. He set out across the oval, a vast plain of green. He took a semicircular path, to avoid the cricket pitch. As he walked he looked down, watching the way his feet slurred through the wet grass. He did not notice one of the boys who, with a laugh to his friends, was rubbing the football in a patch of mud until it was well coated. He did however hear the boy call out "Hey, you!" Startled, James looked up.

As soon as he did the boy, with a huge kick, booted the ball high toward him. James was trapped by it as surely as a horse on a halter. He could not, and did not, move. Instead he stood with mouth open and watched the ball drop. It landed about five meters away from him and began bouncing vigorously, with high adolescent hops. But James still made no move. The ball's energy faded; the bounces became limp and weak.

There was something so pathetic about the ball's wasted contortions that even the boys on the other side of the oval did not move until it finally stopped. But a moment later the boy who had kicked it suddenly began screaming, as though a string had been snapped.

"Pick it up, you little veg!"

James did not respond. He seemed not to understand what was expected of him. His passivity enraged the boy further.

"Pick it up!" he yelled, starting to walk toward James. He received no answer. The boy himself did not speak again, but continued walking, purposefully and silently. The other boys lounged and watched. Some were smiling, some looked bored, a couple seemed concerned, annoyed. Although James trembled as the boy approached he did not move; indeed he did not take his eyes off his face. Time had become stagnant; the boy, without walking faster, continued to stride toward James, pressing the space between them. Then he reached James and with a swing of a clenched forearm knocked him down. James was astounded to find himself lying on the grass. The sky seemed shaken and so did the ground. He looked away from the boy, toward the goalposts at the end of the field. The boy stood over him for a moment, then, frustrated, swore and stamped away to the ball. He

37

had to wipe it clean before he could pick it up but, that done, he gathered it and kicked it to his friends. He ran back to them without another glance at James.

James lay in the grass for some minutes. After a while the ball rolled near him again, this time accidentally. A younger boy collected it then came over and looked curiously at him.

"Are you all right?" he asked.

James did not reply and the boy ran off to his friends, calling, "I think he's retarded or something."

James got up suddenly and walked away. He came to the fence again and doggedly climbed over it. As he crossed Wilson Street he decided that he would walk down the street in huge zigzags, left to right then right to left, then left to right . . .

SOMETIMES I like it like this, and sometimes I don't. Some days are peaceful, some days are bad. On the peaceful days I think the bad days don't matter but on the bad days nothing could be worse. Those are the days I can't sleep and I can't wake. I think about dying and every time I hear and see a word about death I lose my breath and my heart gets heavy and wants to stop. It happens when I hear an ambulance or see a TV show where someone dies or see an advertisement like "Deadly to Insects" or hear a song or catch someone talking about death. I lie in bed and watch the clock and time never passes so slowly while I think about how long it'll be before my turn comes and how bad it'll be.

Once I went into a church. It was so cool and quiet in there. It was like they'd caught nature inside stone. The light fell across the floor in squares of life and death. High above, a fan slowly turned. I walked along the sides, scared to go in the middle or near the front. All along the wall were small sad stories. "Aged 19." "Aged 23." "Aged 8." A man dressed in black came out of one doorway and walked slowly to another. He opened the door there but, changing his mind, closed it and went back out through the first one. I held my breath but he didn't see me.

I slipped along one of the seats, then cut across the central aisle and slid onto a seat on the right hand side. On the board in front of me, but higher than me, were some numbers. I closed my eyes and sat there, wondering when it'd happen to me.

IN THE murky gray of a Melbourne twilight Tiffany found she could not rely on others to keep out of her way. She had to concentrate more than she wanted on the people and obstacles that crowded the footpath. It left little time to think about her client, even though his name flared from every newspaper poster and was shouted by every newsboy's voice. It was not until she was on the tram and able to sink gratefully into an offered seat that she could concentrate on him, and his limited, inevitable future.

"Inevitable," she thought grimly, "if only for political reasons." Americans had become so unpopular with civilians. She had already been told unofficially by powerful friends that there would be no reprieve. There was no sympathy for him as a man and no special circumstances to plead on his behalf.

Funny, she had not expected to be moved herself by any sympathy for him. As the only woman at the Bar she was used to getting unpopular cases. She remembered untying the pink ribbon, in her still, silent chambers, with a sense of hopelessness. Perhaps if she had approached it more positively he might have fared better . . . with this thought she put her head back on the seat and closed her eyes. She wouldn't take any more clients on capital charges. It was too hard to leave the cases behind when you went home at night.

A voice interrupted her: "Excuse me miss, me and me friend were wondering . . ." She opened her eyes. A middle-aged woman with an old coat and shapeless hat was peering into her face. "Were you the lady we saw in court today? With that American fellow, the murderer?"

She nodded and gave a little smile. This happened occasionally.

"My word, you did speak well for him. But the jury didn't take long did they? Fancy you being on the same tram!" Tiffany nodded her head again and closed her eyes, but the voice went on: "Me and me friend, we think he must have been one of them deserters. They do say there's a lot of them up in the bush." Tiffany did not respond. She could not be bothered saying to the woman, as she had already said to her friends, to her colleagues, to the Court, that the American Army had done thorough checks and had no record of him. Whoever he was, he was not one of theirs. But people believed what they wanted to believe. Calling him a deserter was a convenient explanation. And the alternative . . . well, what was the alternative? A confusing, frustrating, clouded riddle.

From the first he had made no effort to assist her. He had not even instructed her how to plead, just shrugged when she asked him. The evidence had been overwhelming, of course. Largely circumstantial, but still overwhelming. The only thing to be said on his behalf was that his victim wasn't much of a loss to society. A string of convictions for sex offenses, and drug importations . . . all small time, but still . . . of course the law, quite rightly, didn't take the moral character of the victim into account . . . as Mr. Justice Adler had said:

"There are circumstances under which the law recognizes that a victim may have contributed to his own fate. But you have chosen to remain silent on this possibility, as you have on a good many other matters. In the absence of any evidence on motive the Court cannot speculate as to mitigating circumstances. Despite learned counsel's eloquent strivings on your behalf, my statutory duty is clear." And he had donned the black cap.

Afterward, at Simpson's request, and ignoring her usual rules, she had visited him in the cell under the courtroom, where he was being held until the crowds dispersed. To her own surprise, she had felt relaxed with him, as though they were suddenly old friends.

"Won't you tell me a little more?" she had asked. He, too, seemed to have changed; for the first time she saw him smile.

"John Simpson," he said, and shrugged.

"No, you're not," she answered. "Who are you really?"

"It doesn't matter," he said. "I just wanted to ask you one thing: are there grounds for an appeal?"

She hesitated, then looked at him levelly. "No," she answered.

"All right," he said. "I expected that. But I wasn't sure about Australian law. Thank you for being straight with me." He paused and then went on, "Ma'am, I do want to thank you for your efforts. I guess I've been a frustrating client, but that's the way it goes." There had been a few more sentences in the same vein, before she made her excuses and left, but he had remained as controlled, as calm, as enigmatic as ever. Now she was unlikely to see him again; now there were only traces left; the memory of his flat New England voice and the cries of the newsboys: "Mystery killer to hang! Mystery killer to hang!"

The sentence was carried out three weeks later: it was 1942 and there was no time for protracted legal affairs. He became a footnote in a dusty law book, quickly forgotten by a public which was becoming sated with headlines of spectacular catastrophes and triumphant victories. Tiffany Guinness remembered him, but naturally enough her memories faded as the years went by.

JAMES SAT in his room. Mr. Woodforde's machine was on the desk in front of him. He was scared of it, but he played with it as though it held no particular power. He switched it on and off a few times, watching the needle on the battery indicator rise slowly from zero to nine, and even slightly beyond nine. "What would happen if the battery went flat while you were away?" James wondered. He drew the machine closer to him, knowing from the burning feeling on his face that he was about to use it again. With sudden carelessness he keyed in random numbers: 45° 25' 15" 45° 25' 15" followed by a date and a time: 11:09. 1948, 1400 hours. Then, before he could have second thoughts, trying to ignore the sick feeling in his stomach, he pressed "Enter."

Again came the terrible glimpse, again the disintegration, with James having time only for one desperate thought: "I shouldn't have done this." He was starting to think, "Why didn't I learn from the last time?" when the insides of his body seemed to fall away and water engulfed him. He was hit by a wave that stung him and drenched him and threw him over. A grim struggle followed, with James' body fighting a fight to which his mind had not adjusted. There was too much to cope with: the shock, the cold, the wet, the salt, the strength of the water. James had to separate each sensation and identify it before he could respond to it. He opened his eyes and found that he was floundering in gray water under a gray sky. Only the white flecks on the tops of the waves enabled him to separate air from water. He was tossed and rolled and knocked from trough to trough, while the cold took possession of his body as though it were a spirit.

Only one thing could save James, and it was the thing that had brought him here. Through it all some kind of desperate reflex had kept his hand gripped around the machine. His fingers were clamped to it with a power that nothing could release. He did not know it was there but he would have known had it not been. As he came flapping and gasping to the surface, for the third or possibly the fourth time, his fingers groped for the keys on the bottom of the panels. But he was rolled under the water again before he could find what he wanted. When he felt air again, nearly a minute later, he had no strength left to sob, or even to breathe. Somewhere deep inside him some instinct forced one frozen frightened finger, taut like a talon, to scratch at the surface of the machine. It felt a key. It pressed, as he was engulfed by a huge gray wave. He was not feeling the cold of the water now, just its weight.

Then that giddying moment of horror emptied him of everything, even himself, until he was suddenly standing, staggering knock-kneed, at the back of an old wooden shed. He didn't care where he was until he had stopped being sick, and then for some minutes more after that. The first thing he noticed, to his relief, was that he was dry—the water had not traveled the years and kilometers with him. The second thing he noticed was that no one was nearby and this was also a relief. And then finally, some minutes later, he started to wonder where he was. But a few steps, to the corner of the building, brought recognition. The old wooden shed was one of the car pool garages, a few hundred meters from Administration. James circled around the back of the Administration building and entered the square through the network of old laboratories. As he passed Lab 17 he gave a quick nervous sideways glance. He was scared of it now. He did not want to go in it or near it, did not want to think about what it looked like, or about any of the moments he had spent in there.

IN THE machine called his memory James went back, back to Mt. Speakman. There had been three days of sleet that stung like wasp bites—cold hard unfriendly little bullets—and fogs, and strong winds. By then they were all ready to go home. "This is no fun," James grumbled to his parents. "Don't worry, it'll clear up," they said each morning.

The first day he had played Monopoly with his sister until nearly lunch time, when they had a gigantic squabble that, in relation to their earlier ones, was like Mayfair compared to Old Kent Road. She had run off in tears and he had gloomily packed the game away, getting no pleasure from his neatly stacked piles of money, nor his glittering array of hotels and houses. In the afternoon he had skied for an hour, but the weather was painful and bitter.

The second day they played cards in the morning and watched videos all afternoon until their heads ached. The third day James met up with friends from school, Peta and Rupert, and went off with them to their flat, leaving Ellie to do . . . what? He tried guiltily not to wonder too much about how she would spend her day. Their parents had gone to the Curlewis' place to play bridge.

But on the fourth day James awoke to the certainty that all the world was either blue or white. Through his window, from his bed, he could see nothing but blue, and when he sat up he found to his delight that the blue was limited only by the white. He sprang out of bed and got straight into his ski clothes before running into the kitchen for breakfast. There was a new mood in the apartment: a mood of lightness and silliness. People made silly jokes and other people laughed immoderately at them.

Ellie had her pink ski suit on, which James privately thought looked revolting, but he told her she was looking good and she beamed. By nine o'clock he was tumbling out of the door, getting his boots and skis in a clatter of noise and excitement. Then, suddenly moved by a moment of compassion, which he knew he would later regret, he said to Ellie, "Come on, El, you want to ski with me?"

He was rewarded by the life that came into her face.

They skied all morning. Fresh powder snow had fallen overnight and they cut through it in laughing sweeping turns and delicate sharp maneuvers. James was longing to go over to Snake Gully and do jumps with his friends but he swallowed his impatience. Most of the time he skied at Ellie's speed, only occasionally bursting into long rhapsodies of genuinely fast movement, then pulling up after a few minutes to wait for her.

Late in the morning he took her down a run that he had found for himself a couple of seasons back, an alternative route down Duke's Drop. It involved a long zigzag through trees, ducking a few times to get under low branches, then a tricky bit through rocks and bushes, ending with a real slalom course through small trees and a jump right next to the bottom of the chairlift. The first couple of times down it Ellie was nervous but she quickly gained confidence and was soon keeping up quite sucessfully.

At about noon he noticed that she was getting wheezy. "This had better be the last run," he said, "then we can go back and have lunch."

"OK, I'm hungry," she said, pushing off. "I'll go first this time."

"OK," James said, watching her lean gracefully into the long turn that took her off the main run and into the trees. "She's getting quite good," he thought, before starting after her. He flicked in and out of the trees casually, then began concentrating on planting his pole as he made each turn. Coming through the small scrubby trees before the jump he had almost caught Ellie, but he was hardly aware of her until he heard a loud crack and the crunch of timber breaking. Looking up he saw that she had failed to duck for the last branch. It had caught her across the top of her head, but she was going too fast to stop. She sailed over the jump out of control, with blood scattering from her scalp. James felt his stomach lurch and his body lurched with it as he lost balance for a moment, then he planted his poles and pushed forward, over the jump.

While he was in the air he took in the scene below, like a snapshot. Ellie lay in a heap of snow and skis and limbs, but she was struggling to get up, despite the blood that was richly marking the snow. People from the chairlift queue were already starting up the slope toward her. James landed and did a tight and fast turn to stop beside her. As he did so he realized with a mixture of fear and relief that his parents were among the half a dozen people coming up the slope. He braced himself for the storm: it came at once.

"What on earth do you think you're doing, bringing her down there?" James' father hissed at him. "What have you done?" he asked Ellie, kneeling beside her. But she was crying too much to answer. Blood was soaking through her hair and running down the back of her head, staining her pink suit.

"Hit my head on a branch," she said at last, between sobs.

"Oh, for God's sake," said James' mother, looking angrily at him. A woman standing with them took her gloves off and began parting Ellie's hair, feeling for the wound. Her hands seemed so experienced that James thought she might be a doctor.

"Not too bad," she said after a minute. "Head wounds always bleed a lot. Might need a couple of stitches, that's all." Ellie gave a fresh little splutter of sobs. James noticed, with new guilt, that she was wheezing worse than ever. "See if you can get a skivvy or a towel," the woman directed, standing up. "Fill it with snow and hold it on her head while you get her to the Medical Center. I think you can get there on your own two legs, can't you?" she said, addressing Ellie. "I don't think you need the ski patrol."

"Have you got your Ventolin?" James' mother asked.

"Yes," Ellie sniffled, groping in her pocket for it.

"I've got a little bag here that might make an icepack," a man said, producing a cloth satchel from inside his parka. He clumsily emptied it of its contents, which ranged from sunglasses to a balaclava.

"That's just the thing," the woman said, as James' father filled it with snow and settled it onto his daughter's head.

"Well, thank you very much, everybody," James' mother said. "You've been most helpful. James should have known better than to take his sister off the groomed runs. Now," she said to the man, "you must tell us where you are staying, so we can return your bag."

"Oh, there's no real need," the man said. "I'm at Michell's chalet, if you happen to be passing, but don't go out of your way. And my name's Herbert, Frank Herbert. You could just leave it at Reception.

"Well, we'll certainly get it back to you," James' mother said. "James can drop it in this afternoon. And now, James," she said, turning to him, "you can go straight over to Running Waters and find the Newcombes and tell them we'll be late for lunch. Tell them we'll drop Ellie at the Medical Center, but they're not to wait for us. You can come back to the Medical Center then and look after Ellie."

James skied down to the chair lift, relieved to be away. He spent the afternoon hanging around the Medical Center, and then baby-sitting Ellie back at the flat. Outside, the sun still shone and the snow was a white dazzle.

"WHEN THE war is over," the girl with the scarred face thought, as she followed her parents wearily through the city, "I'll eat chocolate again. I'll smell coffee. I'll swim in clear clean water." The handle of the bigger bag was cutting intolerably into her left hand, so she paused again to change the bags over. "I wonder how much weight the human body can carry, and for how long?" she thought. "There must be a limit. I wonder if after a while it stretches your bones, or if the muscles tear away from your bones, or what?" She looked up and altered direction slightly, to stay in touch with the weary backs of her parents, a meter or two in front of her.

They were angling across the main square, seeming to dodge by instinct the human traffic: peddlers, beggars, refugees, police and soldiers. A group of nuns hurried past, their faces impassive but their eyes narrowed and concerned. On one of the public buildings a banner still hung, torn by time and twisted by weather. It was no longer possible to read it. Its message, that must recently have seemed so urgent, so important, had been superseded by the counterattack from the south. Nevertheless, the girl tried to read it, to reconstruct the words from the fragments that she could see. At least it was something for her to do, something specific.

She paused again in the middle of the square to change hands. The crowd was getting more dense and for a moment her parents disappeared behind a flurry of gray clothing. The girl gave a start forward, then calmed when the crowd parted and her mother's back came into view, fifty meters away. As she prepared to thread her way through the people again, to shorten the invisible cord to her parents, everything changed. The buildings moved, as though they were not stable and permanent, but instead were made of sand and could be shuffled at will. The ground under her feet shifted and reorganized itself, lifting her as it did so, and causing her to stumble. The sky darkened to gray, and then to complete black. All this happened in the time it took her to drop the heavier bag and open her mouth. Then a moving wall of air and sound hit her and she staggered backward. The sound that came with it deafened her: an earthquake of a sound, a whole world of sound, a Heaven and Hell of noise.

She opened her mouth a little further, to scream or cry out, but any sound she made, even the thought of a sound, was blown away by the noise. She saw that the old clock tower was coming toward her: the fact that the vertical was soon to be horizontal was final proof that the world was being reorganized. If vertical and horizontal could be as one, then three-dimensional could become two, or one, or four, and life could become death. But before the great mass of masonry could reach her she was struck by an absurdly small piece, a lump of brick, a mere harbinger of the building itself. She dropped to the ground, still holding the lighter bag, unconscious before she fell, knowing nothing of the crash as the two planes at last met. She did not feel her body being picked up by the bang of air, nor did she feel the tons of rubble cover her, nor was she aware of the awful airless silence that followed.

She was aware of very little for the next three and a half days.

TWO TEENAGERS named Max and Sybil had arrived to take James out. They did this occasionally. He was not sure who they were or where they came from or why they did it, but he liked their good-humored chatter and their breezy confidence. On this particular day they walked a couple of kilometers to Rymill Park. Max and Sybil talked across his head but also tried to include him in the conversation. Sybil was a girl who moved gracefully and spoke with a light and lively voice; Max was clumsier but good-natured. He often surprised, with comments of real originality.

They were talking about one of their teachers. They went to the same school, a senior high about five kilometers away.

"He's got no sense of humor," Max complained. "Were you there the other day? He told us to choose something in the room and paint it. Those were his exact words. So Andrew Reeve chose the back of the door and started painting it blue. Mr. Angus was so busy cutting up bits of paper that he didn't notice for ten minutes. When he did he went sick at Andrew. Absolutely and completely el sicko. He tried to chuck Andrew out of the class but when he opened the door he got blue paint all over his hands. It was so funny. I had to put my face under the tap to stop myself laughing. But he didn't see the joke at all."

"Strange, that," said Sybil dryly, while James choked back his own laughter. Impassivity, one of his most reliable defenses, was threatening to abandon him.

In the park they played cricket, not very successfully with only three players. But after a while some kids at a barbecue with their parents joined them. That made for a better game but intimidated James, who retreated to the outfield and shook his head shyly when invited to bat or bowl.

They'd been playing for half an hour when Max came to the wicket to bat for the third time. He only had twelve runs from his first two innings, which put him well behind the others. The first ball he got sent him falling back over the trash tin they were using as a wicket, causing much laughter among the kids who had joined them. On the principle of "not out first ball" Max was allowed to keep batting. He played the second ball uneventfully without scoring a run. When the third ball hit a bump in the ground and bounced awkwardly Max tried to hook. In doing so he put his left foot in the trash tin. The shock caused him to lose his grip on the bat, which flew into the fire, while the ball popped up in the air to land in a dish of coleslaw that was sitting on a picnic table. Max overbalanced backward landing with his foot still in the bin and its contents strewn around him.

This was too much for James. He collapsed in helpless laughter, losing control completely. For several minutes he lay on the ground, giggling convulsively. When he finally recovered he lay on his back, gazing at the sky. A ragged mass of cloud was rapidly filling it, from horizon to horizon. His feeling of elation was giving way to fear and embarrassment at his abandonment. At last, however, he forced himself to sit up and look across doubtfully at the others.

They were ignoring him. To his amazement it appeared that they had not even noticed. They were too busy recovering from their own fits of laughter. Max was ruefully holding the cricket ball between thumb and middle finger while he explained and apologized to the owners of the coleslaw. The bin lay on its side on the ground. The bat had been retrieved from the fire: it was propped against a picnic chair, apparently undamaged. Sybil was on the ground, chewing on a piece of grass and still laughing, watching Max.

Relieved, James squatted on his haunches and found his own piece of grass to chew. For some reason he began thinking of a story he had once heard about sneezing. The story explained why people say "Bless you" when somebody sneezes. It had originated in the old days, when people believed that during the split second of the sneeze, the sneezer was off-guard, and the

Devil could enter and take possession of the body. Saying "Bless you" was a defense against Satan; he would be driven out when he heard those words.

Squatting there in the grass under the cloudy sky, chewing on a dry stalk, James whispered, so quietly that he heard himself in his mind rather than through his ears, two words: "Bless me." Then he got up and walked toward the others.

THE TOWN was called Ravenswood. A few dozen people still lived there. Their houses lurked behind patches of scrub or squatted at the end of confusing tracks. The thousands who had lived there in the days of mining madness were represented now by the cadavers of their buildings. Most of these were fenced off, with signs threatening trespassers. In the distance the dust moved like silk, but the town itself was still. Somehow it had taken on the hot dullness of the surrounding bush: the only movement was the susurration of decay.

James climbed through a ragged wire fence into a house that was leaning sloppily to one side and had completely collapsed in the farthest corner. He went timidly up the back steps, testing one to be sure it would not crumble under his feet. There was no door, so he was able to walk into what had been the kitchen. The floor was littered with rubbish and animal droppings. On a wall hung half a cheap calendar and a torn tea towel. A pipe running down the wall led to a broken sink, with one tap still poised at an odd angle above it. In the sink was a smashed beer bottle and a few fragments of soap. James ran his finger along the ledge above the sink. Someone had made that ledge, had carved it out of wood and screwed supports for it. It had taken a few hours perhaps, and made the owner of the kitchen pleased and happy.

James went back into the sunlight and began exploring the garden. Although it was now a sprawling mass of overgrowth it was evident that there had once been order beneath the weeds and wild plants. The skeletons of a few sheds still stood at the end of the long garden but they were covered with creepers.

Later, James walked up the hill to the Ravenswood Cemetery. This was well fenced and in one corner was a group of new graves, topped with red dirt, flowers, and freshly erected headstones. But the rest of the cemetery was old. James avoided the new section and walked through the old. Fewer than half the headstones were still standing but even on those many of the inscriptions were illegible. Some had headstones that were now a pile of rubble. And many had no markings at all. A rectangle of half-bricks, glimpsed among the under-growth; growth; a rusting wrought-iron fence enclosing a mess of weeds; plots where there may or may not have once been a burial. James walked among them slowly, sick at heart. He read all of the texts that could be read. A lot were for children; a lot for men and women in their thirties. Some recorded the awful details of accidental deaths: a drowning; collapsed mine shafts; falls from horses. A woman had been killed in a hotel fire. Some of the inscriptions started with the words, "Pray for the soul of . . . ," and James did. He didn't know whether to be angered or moved by the humble acceptance of death revealed in some of the verses: "The Lord giveth and the Lord taketh away."

One phrase recurred again and again: "Always remembered," or its corollary, "Never forgotten." The sadness struck

James hard. The people for whom these things were written, some of them as recently as forty years ago, seemed to have been badly forgotten, erased by all, lost from the memories of all people.

James was reluctant to leave the cemetery without recognizing these silent forgotten dead. He lingered along the path. Finally he managed to bring to mind a few verses of one of the only hymns he knew. He hummed, in a little croaking voice:

> A thousand ages in thy sight
> Are like an evening gone,
> Short as the watch that ends the night
> Before the rising sun.
>
> Time, like an ever-rolling stream,
> Bears all its sons away;
> They fly forgotten, as a dream
> Dies at the opening day.

My Brother
by Ellie H.

My brother's name is James and he's three years older than me. He's fair-haired, with a part on the left side, and he's about a meter and a half tall. I don't know what color his eyes are because I've never noticed. There's not much else I can say about the way he looks. He's just average. I mean, you never think your brother's good-looking but quite a few girls like him, Jacqui

Squire for one, and Frances Wu for another (don't tell them I said so, though).

James is really dreamy. He gets in trouble for not concentrating and for forgetting things and for not doing things when he's told. His favorite subjects are Science and History, and he likes skiing (he's good at that) and reading and movies and tennis and skateboarding.

Although he can be really annoying (like when he takes my stuff or won't do his jobs or tries to boss me around) I like him 'cos he's kind and he's often very nice to me, considering what a pain it must be to have a little sister. He's still done some awful things to me though, like stirring mashed potato into my coffee and putting Gladwrap over the toilet bowl.

One time he was dinking me on his bike and it didn't have any brakes, so when he wanted to stop he told me to put my foot on the wheel and I didn't understand him so I put my foot in the wheel, in the spokes, and it was a bit of a mess. We both came off.

The trouble with James, though, is you never know what he's thinking. When he's really upset he just goes off on his own and won't talk to anyone. I hate that. He was like that when our other grandmother died.

Another thing about him is that he's good at sharing things (except food!) and he gives me good presents. Last birthday he made me a mobile, with all these people on parachutes floating up and down. It's hanging in my bedroom now. It's great. It must have taken ages and ages to make.

Most of my friends fight with their brothers all the time, and of course James and I have arguments sometimes, but not very often. I think I'm lucky with my brother. All in all he's a pretty good guy and we're good friends.

NANCY LINGERED well behind her mother as they approached the escalators. If she was forced to hold hands on the rippled steel serpentine steps, there was no chance to pirouette or stretch or go skittering up and down. But, although Nancy stood three steps above her mother's cardiganed back, the escalator was too crowded to allow any freedom of movement. It irked Nancy to be so restricted, clammed in by adults. At the bottom of the escalator she took her mother's hand again without a word.

It was all so noisy and crowded and full and wonderful. Nancy wandered through the arcades and around the stores and in and out of the little boutiques. She was connected to her mother throughout it all, at times by touch, at times by a bond of sight and instinct. She had been waiting for this day for months, while they worked their way east, dusty and dry with the heat of the inland plains. Though she was sore and tired, she knew that she would roll the taste of this day around in her mouth for months to come. And so she labored on.

Outside one store she paused and, stretching her head back, looked up at the gleaming building impossibly high above her. It swayed against the clouds, and so did she, watching it. It made her dizzy. It was too much to absorb. She straightened up again and shook her head to clear the confusion, refocusing on the brisk masses of people passing her in the street. Then, suddenly realizing that her mother had disappeared into the throng, she panicked and looked sharply around her. In the crowded distance she thought she saw the familiar gray knitted cardigan, and scurried after it, only to find to her embarrassment that it was a black man in a ski jumper. She looked about her, wondering which way to turn next. She was frightened, not only because she was suddenly alone in the alien city, but because she knew her mother would be angry at their getting separated.

She decided on a likely direction, toward a huge array of neon signs. She hurried toward the store, not recognizing it as one that they had already been in.

At the entrance she stood confused, a whirlpool in a river of people. Another flash of gray sent her rushing into a different shop, but she lost it in a flurry among the crowd. She continued through the store to the rear entrance and, turning right, ran along a narrow, colorful, busy street, dodging between pedestrians. At the next intersection she went with the crowd, which took her to the left. Halfway along the block she passed two policemen who were standing idly, watching the traffic. Having absorbed through her ears, her nose, her skin, her parents' suspicion of policemen, it did not occur to her to ask them for help. She had never known anyone to approach a policeman voluntarily. She ran on, pale-faced and panting.

Within ten minutes she was six blocks away from her searching mother. As her mother scoured the streets in one direction, Nancy giddily floundered in another. She had joined the tide of the lost. Like a microscopic form of sea life, a glimmer at the edge of the wet sand, she was picked up by the hurrying throng, dropped again, picked up and tossed around. As night fell, she collapsed into a bus shelter at the edge of a small park. She closed her dry, sore eyes and sat dully in a corner of the bunker.

I'VE GOT a new game. It's called Frankie. Sometimes I know it's a game and sometimes I don't. But even when I don't, I still do.

Frankie is at nights, outside my window. He watches me when I'm looking at him, and sometimes when I'm not. When I'm getting undressed I turn my back now, so he can't see all of me. Sometimes he tells me to stand closer to him, and I always do, but not for very long, because I get sick of it and he doesn't seem to know what to do next. Other times he makes me break something, or eat something, or throw something away.

When I first realized that Frankie was there, I thought he was friendly. I'm not sure now. He keeps changing his expression. You could never call it friendly, though some days he doesn't seem to mind. He reminds me of someone, I don't know who.

Frankie talks to me and knows what I think. Of course it's only a game, but still. And it's only at nights. In the daytime he's so different. He's still there, sort of, but his nose is the end of a branch, where it's been sawn off, and his mouth is leaves, and his eyes are the buds on the ends of twigs. I look at all those bits then and try to imagine how they could be a face at nights, but it's hard. I can sort of see it, but only when I try, and it doesn't work much then. You know how you see a photo of your parents when they're young? You look and you look and you can just see the traces of them in their faces as kids, but you have to concentrate. You can't look away. That's how it is with Frankie.

When I'm in a good mood I joke around with Frankie and I deliberately try to scare myself. Because, don't forget, I know he's not real. When I'm in a bad mood he scares me though. He looks mean. He won't let me off.

I know Frankie'll keep changing and eventually he'll fade away. The leaves will spread or the bough will grow or the buds will flower. I know it'll happen, and it'll be good then, but in a way I don't want it to. I'm sort of comfortable with old Frankie. He's someone to have there, someone to hang around with. He's my face at the window.

MR. WOODFORDE'S machine had acquired a kind of horror in James' eyes. The sense of disintegration he experienced when he used it was so frightening that he had trouble nerving himself to handle the machine at all. He began to wonder if he had left a bit of himself behind each time he came back from the past. He felt that he was not being reassembled quite correctly. Parts of him did not seem to match up properly. When he took a shower he gazed solemnly in the bathroom mirror, convincing himself that his nose was off-center, and there were too many gaps between his teeth, and one nipple was bigger than the other.

Nevertheless, he felt obliged to use the machine. He knew he had access to an extraordinary power. He felt it would be a waste not to use it, almost a crime. He was sure that if anyone else had it they would be using it all the time. So on a quiet Sunday afternoon, the day after going to the park with Sybil and Max, he forced himself to go through the procedures again.

This time he was more organized. Although his real interest was in people and events that had personal meaning for him, an obscure sense of duty urged him to undertake a "proper" historical exploration. It was as though his teacher, Mrs. Chalmers, was in the room and looking over his shoulder. He felt obliged to go back into history. He had always been fascinated by the Mayans. He had done a school project on them, read a few books about them and had a picture of their temples on his wall. So when he had to choose a place it seemed obvious that it should be Central America. After some study he decided on 16° 50' 0", 90° 0' 0". For a date he chose A.D. 795, arbitrarily nominating June 16 at 1130 hours.

His research through books and maps told him that this should take him to the ancient city of Tikal, in Guatemala. And with little further thought—and with no thought for any practical difficulties—he sat at his desk and started keying in the date.

It was fear of the sensations that he must once again experience that filled his mind. The fear crowded through his awareness, pushing all else to the corners, then crowding into the corners, too, till there was no room left. And when at last he pressed the "Enter" button he was disgusted to find that his fears and memories were not exaggerated. It was an awful, lurching experience again, that this time lasted for several minutes. When it was over, he was too dizzy and sick to see or care where he was, until three or four more minutes had passed. Then he began to notice things.

He realized that the air was different. It was rich and sweet, flooding the senses. He was standing among trees, looking out at a vast city. It was full of exotic stone buildings gleaming in the morning sun. A hubbub of noise, human noises, was beating away steadily, though he could not quite see its origin. But a step forward gave him a better view, over a stone wall, and he saw a kind of market spread in front of him. He was first struck by the number of people in it, then by how different they looked. For one thing, they seemed small. No one here to rival the tall

Americans at the Research Center, or even his tall father, the Director. For another, they were all very brown, their skin glowing with a tan that might have been enhanced by oil. The men wore headdresses and cloths that were tied around their waists and between their legs. The women had dresslike shifts and long hair tied back. The children seemed to wear the same costume as the men, though some were naked.

The noise was terrific. There was shouting and laughter and chatting and arguments. Some kind of nobleman, more elaborately dressed, was carried past in a litter. A doglike animal, tied to a stake in the ground, was being fed by a child. James began to notice details, to sort out the full and complicated picture that was before him. Goods were spread across the ground and on stalls, from one corner of the concourse to the other, and people wandered among them comparing, examining, negotiating. He saw a man buying a small woven basket from among a collection tied to a pole, and James strained to see how he paid for it. Something changed hands—perhaps some small coins— but he could not see what they were. He started to look more closely at the array of goods on display. They seemed to be mainly foods of all kinds. Fruits, beans, seeds, carcasses of freshly killed animals, smoked meats, herbs in baskets. Many were varieties that he did not recognize but others were familiar. Some were obviously types of bread and there were many kinds of melon, pineapples, avocados, strawberries, and tomatoes. As well, he recognized potatoes, sugar cane, and sweet corn.

Yet many of these foods were different in shape, size, and color from the way James knew them. The pineapples and tomatoes, in particular, were smaller than the ones from the Defense Forces' canteen. The tomatoes were more orange than red. There were rabbits hanging in a shaded corner of the concourse, but they had dark tails and long ears, and they looked quite big.

James turned his attention to his own position. He was standing among rich, dark, exotic trees in an uncleared patch of rain forest or jungle. The wall in front of him was about chest high. Made of stone, it seemed old and neglected. Although it was cool among the trees, the early morning freshness was starting to go, and the sun was beating onto the paved road of the marketplace. Insects, mainly mosquitoes, were beginning to find James and to swarm around him.

He took another step forward, a little further out of the shade and shelter. At last a realization of his difficulties began to dawn on him. He was wearing blue denim jeans and a T-shirt with a frog on it. He was blond, fair-skinned, blue eyed: the complete opposite of these people. He spoke English and no other language. Starting to sweat, he looked down at his hand, seeking visual reassurance of what he was holding in a tight grip: Mr. Woodforde's machine. He moved it slightly, so that his thumb was better placed to hit the "Return" button if things got out of control. Then he took a deep breath and walked to the wall.

He expected to be noticed at once, but because the wall came up so high on his body he was still concealed from the marketplace. He waited a moment, then put the machine on top of the wall to free his hands, levered himself up, grabbed the machine, and dropped to the ground on the other side.

For the few seconds that this took he did not have time to look at the people in the marketplace, but as he landed on the stone pavement, facing the wall, he felt a prickling in his back and a dryness in his throat. He gripped the machine even more tightly, taking care to align his thumb with the "Return" button again, before turning to face the Indians.

A silence had descended over the market: a silence so sudden and complete that it was hard to believe a clamor of voices had filled the air a moment earlier. Sweating all over now, not just in his hot hands and wet armpits, James looked up at the Mayans.

They were all frozen, all quiet, gazing at him. Most had drawn together, had sidled across to each other, so that James was now standing alone. One, a man of about twenty, still on his own, caught James' eye and quickly, almost guiltily, scuttled into a group. A large highly colored bird suddenly flapped into the sky from a wall behind a pottery stall. Triggered by its movement a number of similar birds arose from other points along the concourse and flew to join it. They clustered and perched on a branch of a tree away to James' left.

The machine, and its silent assurance that it could extricate him instantly, gave James some confidence. Not a lot, but some. He moved a meter forward. There was no response among the Indians. Even a baby, about twelve months old, sitting on the ground nearby, gazed at him with unwavering concentration. James took another step. Then, to his own surprise, in a high, nervous voice, he said:

"I don't want to cause any trouble. My name's James. I just wanted to visit you."

Here and there various spectators exchanged glances. James knew they could not understand his words but he was hopeful that they might understand the tenor of his message. He waited for a minute to see if anything would happen, but there was still no movement. So he walked to where the baby sat, and patted its head. A woman standing nearby emitted a low slow hiss. The baby, for no apparent reason, started crying. James, watching the crowd intently, still gripping the machine, went to a small cooking fire beside an array of food. He selected a sweet potato, picked it up and bit into it. Someone in the crowd called out. There was a murmur, and a shifting of feet. Suddenly a boy ran forward. He looked younger than James, but because of the small build of these people it was hard to tell. He stood a meter from James, gazing with a startled look into his face. He seemed startled at his own impetuosity. The two boys locked eyes and stared in fascination and fear at each other. James noticed that the boy was holding a knife and, realizing that he might not re-act fast enough if the boy went to stab him, he nearly pressed the "Return" key there and then. But he resisted the tempta-tion. He wanted to break the intense eye contact but was scared to, thinking that it might be interpreted as a sign of weakness. Instead he groped with his right hand for another sweet potato and, finding one, brought it up between the two of them. With-out taking his eyes off the other boy he took a bite out of the vegetable and then handed it to the Mayan. Slowly, after a long, long pause, the boy bit a large piece out of it with his clean white teeth, then chewed and swallowed.

There was a roar from the onlookers. The tension had been broken by this simple act. People started to move toward them. James, fearful of being mobbed, held up his hand, and the movement stopped. He grinned at the boy. The Indian looked at him without smiling, but James was reassured by the lively in-telligence of his dark eyes, just as he was struck, incongruously, by the largeness of the boy's nose. The boy pointed toward the southern end of the concourse and said something in his own language. He took a few steps in that direction, indicating that James should follow. James saw no harm in doing so. The two boys began walking through the Indians, weaving in and out of the colorful market display. Most people stood their ground as they passed; a few stepped back a little, a few reached out a hand and touched James curiously. He was embarrassed, but also exultant.

They left the market, skirting around a number of two-story stone and plaster buildings, and started out along a vast arena with huge pyramids at the end of it. James gaped at the scale of it all. Behind him he became aware that the crowd had fallen into line, and more people were joining all the time. He checked again that the machine, now finely laced with drops of his sweat, was still in his hand. He even quickly flicked it on to check the battery indicator, and was relieved to see that the needle went to seven.

The pyramids, fronted by giant staircases and topped by ornate structures that looked like tombs or altars, were looming closer. The boys passed complex carved slabs of stone. The crowd behind them seemed to be hesitating, falling back. But the Mayan boy led on confidently. He went within fifty meters of several of the biggest pyramids without looking at them. At last a possible destination was revealed to James by the focus of the boy's eyes and the undeviating course of his walk. They seemed to be aiming at a smaller building at the edge of the plaza: again made of stone and windowless, resembling a couple of huge coffins of different sizes, piled on top of each other. As they came closer James realized that the building was beside a hole some ten meters in diameter. A few people stood at regular intervals around the hole, but no one else seemed to be nearby. They were all men, dressed more elaborately than the people in the market. Their costumes were fuller around the waist and they wore spectacular headdresses, which, in their rich plumage of feathers and leaves, blended easily with the background of the dense green jungle that pressed so close to the end of the plaza.

The men, who had dark skin and large noses like James' guide, looked steadily and impassively at James for a minute, then, without moving from their places, began questioning the Indian boy. His answers were brief but given without hesitation. The men turned their attention to James again and indicated that he should stand on a certain spot, close to the edge of the hole. Feeling increasingly fearful he nevertheless obeyed. As he stepped to the new position one of the men moved in behind him and stood very close, up against his back. James could now see that the crowd had stopped some distance away and was hushed. All were watching. He was startled to see how many people there were.

Looking down, he saw that he was standing on the edge of some kind of natural well. A smell of mold and mildew filled it. He could see green water about twenty meters below. Although it was dim and in shadow he thought there were large objects, dark and bulky, breaking the surface of the water. A few meters away, to his left, a sudden clatter and shriek startled him horribly and he jerked and looked around, heart jumping. It was a bird, glaringly golden and black, but quite small. It flew rapidly out of some vines and across the pool in front of him, beating its wings noisily.

Before he had even looked away another startling and horrible cry came to him. This time it was unmistakeably human. It came from the well at his feet. Rigid with astonishment he looked down. He thought he saw a face in the water, perhaps looking up at him. Though he had never heard the shriek of a drowning man he had not a moment's doubt as to the meaning of this cry. He became taller, and whiter, stretching and gazing down with open mouth at the green mysteries in the shadowy hole. He looked across at the face of his young guide, searching for a clue, a lead. The boy looked back at him guileless, interested, alert. James started to twist around to say something, though he was unsure of what the words would be, but the man behind him placed a heavy hand on each of his shoulders and kept him weighed down on the spot. The man spoke; clear, loud words in a deep and dark voice. It sounded like a proclamation. James, obscurely, felt obliged to play his part. He stood still, half-listening to the wise voice. Then, suddenly, the man pushed him hard in the back, and he fell.

Falling, jerking, falling, his stomach still up at the brink: he saw a circle of blue, and dark shapes, then dim soft green. He was dropping into smell. The whole thing was too astonishing to understand. The only emotion was fear. No thinking, just feeling, and the only feeling fear. He hit the water but it was not all water: he half-landed on something soft and bulgy, with hard lines in it. He understood that it was human, a body. Suddenly he was grabbed with manic force: an arm clamped across his chest and a fierce, desperate, dark face, with a big nose, was staring into his. James' mouth, his whole face, was open wide with horror. His face was in the shape of a scream but no sound came. The man was pressing him down, pushing and forcing him down. James was drowning in a silent struggle. He could not seize on a single thought that might save him. There was no room for that, just for gaping unformed fear. His face was under the water twice, three times. The man had ceased to be a human, if indeed he had ever been one. Now he was a force, an idea, evil. James floundered.

As he had known in the ocean, so again he knew in a part of his mind that there was something that could save him. It was not a considered, rational thought but he knew there was something, and it was in his hand, and it was the key to his survival. A part of him that was not dying struggled with this knowledge. A persistent voice told him to press. Press? Press what? It doesn't matter, just press. He pressed. Nothing happened. With no air left, nothing left, he went under again. The lights in his head focused themselves, concentrated, then began to resolve themselves into one bright coin of light. Then the light, while not fading in brightness, began to withdraw in distance, to travel away from him, at a faster and faster pace. It was a bright strong distant spot, becoming a pinpoint. "Wrong finger," James thought, if it was a thought. He gave a faint, flickering tremble of his thumb.

He was lying on hard earth. It was dark until he realized his eyes were closed. He did not open them for quite some time. He was frightened of what he might see. When he did open them he saw an apple tree in the backyard of the house in which he lived. He lay there a long time, eyes closed, breathing deeply, in a kind of sleep. Afterward he got up and went into the house. The woman who was there said to him, "James! Where have you been? We wanted to go to Grandma's but we couldn't find you. So Daddy's gone on his own." He went upstairs like an old man. As he came to his sister's room he moved across and passed by on the other side of the corridor, looking down at the floor.

JAMES SAT on a swing in the playground, rocking rhythmically to and fro. It was rare for him to get a swing to himself but at the moment the craze was yo-yos and most of the kids were absorbed in them. Some days the rocking motion of the swings made him sick; other days it was restful. Today it felt good.

A little way off were Ellie's old friends, most of them anyway. He watched them covertly. They seemed to be having fun. He wondered how they could and was angry that they were.

It had been raining hard most of the morning and the rain looked as though it was likely to start again soon. Large brown puddles lay morosely around the playground. James studied the one at his feet, then began kicking loosely at it, enough to disturb it violently but not to scatter it. Then he stopped suddenly, noticing a struggle in the water. He looked more closely and realized that he had washed a small insect into the puddle. It was fluttering its water-heavy wings frantically, trying to escape. James watched it for a moment, then used the edge of a dead leaf to lift the insect clear. He put it on dry ground, but the black and gold creature, waterlogged, moved only feebly. James felt that there was nothing more he could do for it. He left it there to dry out and wandered away from the swing, back toward the school buildings. He walked along, thinking of the religious people in India whom he had heard about—the ones who took care, whenever they moved, to harm nothing. Even ants were safe from their light footfalls. James wondered whether the invention of the microscope, and the discovery of all the teeming microscopic life in the world had changed their attitudes. Did they know that

every time they moved they destroyed masses of minute creatures? Just to live was to cause pain.

Coming from the classroom block was Dr. Matheson, a
teacher whom James liked. James was approaching the buildings
at a tangent: he had circled from the swing around the back of
the boys' toilets. Nevertheless, their paths were going to cross.
He became nervous as the encounter grew closer. But he
stopped when they met, and stood looking at the ground.

"Hello, James," Dr. Matheson said in her husky voice. "I've
got something here I thought you might be interested in."

James looked up and saw a small flat object in her hand. She
held it out to him and he took it. It was a maze, three-dimensional,
fully enclosed, containing a metal ball which had to be guided
through many objects and traps to reach a central spot. It ap-
pealed to James, who liked challenges of a mechanical kind. He
smiled. Dr. Matheson was delighted.

"Take it," she said. "Keep it for a few days, or until you're sick
of it. Later I'll give it to my niece. She enjoys that kind of thing,
too."

James walked on, clutching it to his chest. He bypassed the
classroom and went to the janitor's cupboard. Knowing that the
class after lunch was Divinity and he would not be missed he
stayed there until his next lesson, at 2:15.

"WHEN THE war is over," the girl thought, "I will lie under a tree
chewing on a piece of grass. I will kick a pebble along a street. I
will plant a flower garden and water it and keep it free of weeds.
I will smell ripe peaches."

She closed her eyes again, hoping that the next time she opened them she would not see only darkness, only cold and hard rock. Her leg hurt a lot but the hurt had settled into a dull ache, instead of the spectacular flaring pain that had savaged her for many hours. She preferred the dull ache.

SHE HAD been hungry for a while but the hunger passed. She did not know how long she had been there but thought it had probably been all day. The worst thing, perhaps, was the silence, which was terrible.

She passed into a kind of sleep again. If anything had happened she would have been aware of it. But nothing happened. She slept because there was nothing else to do.

DOUG MOTTRAM was a tall, balding man, a solicitor who lived in the city, drove a Saab, and loved to windsurf and play squash. He was married to Cathy and was the father of a son, Andrew.

Cathy Mottram was a tall, clear-skinned woman, a dentist who lived in the city, drove a Volvo, and loved to ride horses and play squash. She was married to Doug and was the mother of a son, Andrew.

One day Cathy had to drive across town to a nursing home to treat an elderly patient with a toothache who was too frail to travel to her. On the way, by arrangement, she picked up Andrew as he came out of school. Andrew sat in the car and did his homework while his mother went into the nursing home. Afterward Cathy drove back through the city, stopping at a medical supply company to purchase some goods. She parked at a meter about half a block away, telling Andrew again to wait in the car.

Cathy was away about ten to twelve minutes. When she returned Andrew had gone.

"Was anything missing from the car?"

"His lunchbox. A street directory."

"Where did he keep his lunchbox?"

"Well, it was normally in his schoolbag, which was still in the car. But his lunchbox wasn't in it anymore, so we assume that's when it went missing."

"Did he seem upset about anything?"

"No, quite the contrary."

"Was he the kind of boy who might run away?"

"No, he's a happy, confident child."

"Has he ever run away?"

"Oh, just the usual tantrums when he was younger. He went round the block a couple of times."

"Did you have any arguments during the car trip?"

"No. He was keen to get his homework done before we got home, so he could watch television. That seemed to be his major concern."

"When's the last argument you had with him?"

"Oh . . . I suppose . . . on Monday. I wouldn't let him go to his friend's place, because he'd been there half the weekend anyway. I said it was Jem's turn to come here. It wasn't a major argument—he could see the sense of it. He's a sensible kid."

"Was he in any trouble at school?"

"No, he's quite a leader there, it seems. The teachers like him."

"Would he have left the car with a stranger voluntarily?"

"Heavens, no."

73

"Did you see anyone you knew during the afternoon's driving?"

"No, not really. I mean just the usual parents and kids outside the school. And there were a few staff and patients at the rest home whom I've gotten to know over the months I've been going there."

"Do you have any enemies?"

"Oh, not like that, no."

"Anybody who might wish you harm?"

"No, no."

"Is he a healthy boy?"

"Oh yes."

"No bumps on the head lately? No concussions or similar?"

"Not that we've heard, or know about."

Doug and Cathy Mottram continued searching for their son when after ten days it became clear that the police had no leads and no idea of what might have happened. They did streetwalks, and doorknocks, and distributed photographs and posters. Gradually their search widened, across the state, across the country. They became increasingly desperate. They agreed that Doug would take leave from his practice, indefinitely, but Cathy would keep working. It was the only way they could get the money to finance the enormous expenses they were incurring. They hired a private detective. Doug traveled ceaselessly, investigating reported sightings that came in at regular intervals. Andrew had been seen in a McDonald's in Williamstown. He'd been spotted hitchhiking on the Lawrance Highway. He was with a man in Semmler. He'd been killed in a road accident in Laing. He was in a youth refuge on the East Side. As far as

Doug could ascertain, none of the reports was true. Under the strain of Andrew's disappearance the marriage began to break up. Both Doug and Cathy began drinking too much. They seemed unable to talk to each other about their fears, their grief. They steadily drifted apart. Eventually Doug moved into a small apartment about five kilometers from what had been the family home. About six months after the separation he attempted suicide, by taking an overdose of sleeping tablets. He was found by his brother, and taken to hospital in good time.

A year after that Doug was in a small town called St. Antony, on the north coast. He was staying with new friends. Jane was an airline hostess. Doug met her on one of his many flights in search of Andrew. On a near-empty plane they had talked. She had taken a sympathetic interest in the father's quest for his son. He had met her again a number of times, and then met her husband, Raffael, a photographer. Now he was staying with them for a weekend, at their beach house.

On the Saturday evening the three of them were fishing off the beach and made a series of big strikes. Doug, in particular, caught the biggest fish of his life: a beautiful full-bodied bream. Raffael went up to the house to get a camera, then photographed Doug as he proudly held the fish aloft in the dusk.

A week later the photos from Raffael came in Doug's mail. He opened them and looked through them with pleasure: the warm rising of good times remembered. The third and fourth photos were of the fish. There was not much difference between them which was not surprising, as they were taken only a few moments apart. But there was one important difference. The second of the two photos contained an extra person in the background. Peering out from under Doug's outstretched arm, about a meter behind him, was the unmistakeable face of his son, Andrew.

JAMES AND Ellie had to do the shopping while their mother was in hospital. They enjoyed it, feeling important. They spent all the time in the supermarket alternately arguing and giggling. Ellie wanted Coco Pops but James became sanctimonious and insisted on Weet-Bix. Ellie sulked for a while but cheered up when James agreed that they could each have a bar of chocolate. They got serious as they went through the check-out but then clowned around in the Mall for a while before going out to get a taxi home. Their favorite taxi driver, a big Fijian named Eric, was nowhere to be seen, so they took the first cab on the rank, with a driver who hardly spoke to them.

At home Ellie was getting wheezy and went onto her pump for a while. Watching Ellie's face buried in the mask and the steam made James nervous. He went outside and took a few desultory shots at the hoop with the basketball, interrupting himself only to throw the ball at the cat when it stalked past, tail arrogantly aloft. He mooned about for twenty minutes or so, then wandered back into the house. He found Ellie more settled, and reading. James began to make himself a sandwich.

"What are you reading?" he demanded.

"Unfinished Tales," she answered, still focusing on the book.

"Read me some," he said.

She now paid him more attention. "You want me to read you some?" she asked.

"Yes," he said, as he spread marmalade onto the bread.

"From the start?" she asked, rifling back through the pages.

He knew she loved reading to an audience. "No, just anywhere," he said. "Wherever you're up to."

He sat at the breakfast bar as she started to read. "'They were traveling through Nailwood,'" she began. She paused a moment to establish her breathing. "'Ahead of them were three riders, but as the road began to twist into the uplands the riders were quickly lost to view. Sidetracks tempted them with soft green turf, but when Naomi tried to edge off onto one of the tracks it writhed and hissed, and the green turned into the mottled brown and yellow back of a serpent. She leaped back quickly onto the main path.'"

"Holy gooby," said James. "What kind of a book is this?"

"It's a strange one," said Ellie. She looked at him steadily, without a smile.

"It sure is," said James. "I'd like to see them make a movie of it. OK, keep reading."

"'Creepers occasionally scratched lightly past their bodies. Naomi was startled by their teeth, and by their eyes. They had dozens of eyes, of differing sizes, spaced evenly along their length, and when one blinked, they all blinked. Caught in many of their teeth were threads of clothing, strands from earlier travelers.

"'The higher the track climbed, the mushier it became. Puddles of mustard-brown water formed in the flatter sections; they sucked and steamed whenever a foot came close to them. At one point the travelers had to walk through a cloud of insects: big, black, slow-moving winged creatures the size of small birds. Naomi covered her face grimly and battled on.

"'The end came unexpectedly. The track widened onto a pasture. The wind shuddered around the small, rocky expanse and trees teetered at its edges. As they arrived a tree lost its last grip and fell a thousand meters, onto a huge pile of bleached tree bones at the foot of the cliff. So far was its fall that they heard no sound of its impact.

"'The further they moved onto the plateau the more they realized that it was eroding constantly. Rocks slipped and tumbled from its sides, trees toppled with ghastly sighs down the cliff faces, powdered earth blew from the rocky surface.

"'In the center of this plain of constant movement was a still eye. Three white gravestones stood there: dull, cracked, worn, but firm and straight. The travelers struggled toward them. The sky moved and groaned. Naomi's face was gray with knowledge. She bent and read the first one, then the second, then the third. She stepped back. "What do they say?" her companions asked. "I can't tell," Naomi answered, "what they say. The words keep changing. The first one was either . . . I don't know . . . either 'Greed' or 'Grief.' The second one . . . either 'Ignorance' or 'Innocence,' and the third one . . . I can't tell . . . perhaps 'Hate.' Or perhaps 'Hope.'

"'The three stood helplessly in the listening air. Minutes passed. Then Naomi noticed a small bush at the crumbling edge of the plateau. Its small white flowers trembled as the roots of the bush were exposed by the scattering soil and dropping rocks. Naomi ran to it and repacked stones and dirt around it, making the bush secure. At last, having succeeded in her self-appointed task, she stood up. Amazingly, it took her a moment to notice that everything had changed.'"

Ellie seemed to have paused.

"Everything had changed?" James repeated.

"That's all there is," Ellie said.

"That's all there is?"

"Yes." Ellie showed him the blank page in the book. James raised his eyes and corrugated his forehead.

"What kind of book is that?" he asked again.

"Well," Ellie said, "it's full of these little stories and they all seem to link together but I'm not sure how, or what they mean. For instance, the one before this was about a city where everybody lives in parks and they go into houses to play. But then people start to demolish the houses. So Naomi and her friends take the timber and plant it in the ground and water it until it grows back into trees."

"Gee," said James. "Full of opposites."

A car came up the driveway and James stood and peered out the window.

"Dad," he said. Ellie closed the book and took it to her room. James went into the rumpus room and turned on the TV.

FEELING HANDS under her armpits, hard hands that dug in and poked her, the girl squirmed and opened her eyes. The daylight hurt her eyes so she closed them again. Then the pain of her leg engulfed all other pain: it swept her away on a private river, until she was aware of nothing else.

When next she was conscious of the world she found herself in a bed, a hospital bed, with a nurse standing over her. The nurse was mouthing words. The girl could hear the sound of a voice but could not make out any of the words. With the weight of a hundred years on her eyelids she wearily slipped back into sleep.

JAMES SAT on a wall, watching a group of off-duty military men. They formed a circle around an area covered with old bricks and building material. Armed with crowbars they were levering rubble away, flushing out the rats who had been harboring there for many months. From time to time, as a rock was prised away, there was a storm of wild movement: a rat with nose pointed forward and fur flattened dashed through the cordon. About a third of them got away but most were smashed to a halt under the heavy blows of the bars. Some died in a silent thud, some died in a squealing threshing of broken legs and bloody squirming.

James did not know what to think. He hated and feared the rats. Whenever he saw one scurrying around the ground, with its curious mixture of arrogance and furtiveness, he felt sick, and would shake for a long time. But the wild killing of the creatures frightened him, too. They were too big for such slaughter.

Another rat was rolling in the dust while men, with excited cheers, struck it. James ran from the spot. He zigzagged through some tired weedy-looking trees and then made his way among a few older buildings, until he was at Mr. Woodforde's lab. The door was closed and barred, with a padlock through the clasp. The padlock was large and looked strong but when James poked at it he saw that it was a trick: the two parts were joined together but not locked. He opened it, took it off, then opened the door and went in.

The room was dull and dusty. Though few of Mr. Woodforde's possessions remained, nothing new had been added. The impression was one of emptiness, bareness, and cobwebs. James circled the room gingerly, his heart beating a little faster and a little louder. He ran a finger through dust, liking the line it left but uncertain of how to finish the design he had started.

Reaching the front desk where Mr. Woodforde had done most of his work, James pulled out his old stool and sat on it. He gazed around him. It was like being at the museum and seeing the skeleton of a dinosaur. This room was the bones of a life, the dead outline of something that once had flesh, movement, a lively eye. James had been told in Social Studies of the tribute to Christopher Wren, written over the door of St. Paul's Cathedral: "If you would see his monument, look around." He remembered it now, and sighed. There was no monument here, perhaps no monument anywhere to his friend. It occurred to him that he did not even know where the scientist was buried. In the dust he wrote: "I am James, I am me." There was a mirror on the wall, which he went and gazed into for several long minutes, until his face grew unfamiliar to him. He began to think that if he stayed there long enough he would see Mr. Woodforde's face looking back at him from the mirror. He drew away nervously, but a little reluctantly.

On his way out of the lab James paused to examine the notice board near the window, where Mr. Woodforde had pinned various notes and reminders. Nothing much was left on it now except a calendar, a yellowing memo from the Security Department about nighttime movement around the Center, and a newspaper photograph of a one-legged high jumper. The calendar was three years out of date but James took it down anyway and thumbed through it, for the sake of seeing Mr. Woodforde's handwriting again. Sure enough there were occasional notations on it: a dental appointment, a committee meeting, a lecture by a man named Tipler. James finished his desultory scanning and prepared to pin the calendar up again, but as he did so something on the back of it caught his eye. He turned it over and read with pleasure the familiar writing:

> It matters not how strait the gate,
> How charged with punishments the scroll,
> I am the master of my fate:
> I am the captain of my soul.

James set off slowly for his house, closing the lab door behind him. His mind was crowded with images: the rats, the bare room, the poem. He was confused.

GILES GREW slowly in the suburb of Elmo. His father was an accountant and his mother a kindergarten teacher. His first memory was of a tree, in the garden across the road, being struck by lightning. It was a vicious storm. Giles heard the thunder ripping apart the sky but did not know until the next morning that the tree had been split. He went across the road and fingered the burned trunk in wonder. Uneasy thoughts came to him and he returned home to find his blanket.

His blanket was pink and had a name. It was called Zella, though no one knew where the name was from. The blanket had been Giles' companion and solace for a long time. He was so attached to it that it was wearing away: it had become dirty and torn. Every time his parents washed Zella, Giles had made a scene, until eventually they cut the blanket in two. Then, while one half was being washed, Giles could comfort himself with the other half. He hugged it and held it and dragged it behind him.

Many things defined Giles. His build, for instance, his appearance. At nine he was a meter sixteen tall, which was small for his age. One doctor said he was a "failure to thrive" kid. He had brown hair and hazel eyes and was a good-looking child: not an arresting face but a pleasant one. There was an alertness about him that suggested intelligence. He was a Gemini; his hobbies were playing pool, collecting keys, reading, and swimming. He liked computers. When he grew up he wanted to be an engineer or a sports commentator or an Air Force pilot.

He loved his dog, Choof, a sort of shocked-looking terrier. He loved, he supposed, his parents, yet there were things he said and did that made it seem he might not like them very much. He had no brothers or sisters. Both his grandfathers were dead, and one of his grandmothers. The other grandmother lived nearby; she was a formal, well-mannered lady who did not converse easily. She spent a lot of time watching current affairs programs on television.

Apart from his blanket, which became less important to him as he grew older, Giles' favorite possessions were a painted egg that had belonged to his grandfather, a wounded Teddy Bear named Jed, and a pair of bookends. He had bought the bookends with his own money at a fete. Each bore a figure, which appeared to be reaching toward the other through the books.

At school Giles' best subjects were Math and Sport, though he also liked Cooking, which they did every second Tuesday. He was learning to play piano and had passed his Grade One exams.

His best friends were Hamish Woodholme and Ben Jefferson and Georgie Hatcher. His teacher was Mrs. Collinson: Giles thought she was all right.

Giles didn't think about God much, taking it for granted that He existed. He thought about a lot of other things though. He wished he would be elected as a kind of world President who could get everyone to stop fighting and restore the planet to the best possible condition. But he got really bored and annoyed by politicians on TV. He wondered if his parents were really his parents, or if he might have been adopted when he was a baby. He wondered when he'd reach puberty and if he'd have pimples and if he'd be big and tough. He imagined he was the world's best skateboarder, doing handplants and McTwists in front of huge crowds. When he crossed roads at traffic lights he pretended he was a racehorse, and so were all the other pedestrians, and they were racing to be first to the other side, and he usually won, except when he was with his mother or someone he knew, and then he couldn't play that game.

When eating licorice allsorts Giles always took them apart, layer by layer, and ate the licorice first, so he could enjoy the candy parts without black interruptions.

The deepest, biggest thought in Giles, however, was something so bleak and frightening that he could never look at it. He knew it was there: always there. Like his dreams, like his doubts, like his lies, it occupied a large part of him. It was a sense of being incomplete, of there being something missing. It yawned inside him, gaping most hungrily when he was alone or tired or cold or scared, but always there.

Giles didn't understand. He never understood, even when he saw the photograph of the two babies, even when he found a birth certificate with a strange boy's name on it and a photocopy of another birth certificate with it. He didn't understand why the certificates bore his own birthdate. He didn't understand how the two babies could be the children of the same parents.

Giles kept telling himself that it didn't matter, that it was nothing, that he'd ask about it some day. He never did ask and he never quite understood.

GISELLE GREW and grew in the small coastal town of Casterton. She moved quickly through the events of each day, gobbling one before rushing to another. Nothing seemed to satisfy her. She roamed through the moments: as she stood in one her eyes were looking for the next.

She played games with her shadow. She tried to jump away so quickly that she and it would be separated for an instant, perhaps longer. She sidled into the shade of buildings, watching her shadow being gradually taken from her. Walking down the street she would spin suddenly around, hoping to catch her shadow by surprise as it tried to slip away.

Giselle liked some of her parents' old music, like Simon and Garfunkel, and the Beatles, and the Supremes. She wished they hadn't all broken up. Giselle played piano and had passed her Grade Two exams: and she went to Jazz Ballet on Wednesdays after school. As well as music she liked Math and Sport and the few Science lessons that they had.

Although Giselle had no sisters or brothers she had a family of her own. This consisted of Tatlow, a large round toy echidna; Stocky, a purple hippopotamus who was coming apart at the seams; Loretta, a Barbie doll; an injured Teddy Bear named

Jed, who looked disgruntled and had been degrunted; Louisa McKnight, a nineteenth century doll of Giselle's mother's; and Chippy, a black and white elephant. Each night Giselle had to choose which of her family could fit into bed with her: there was only room for one. She was scrupulously fair, making sure they took it in turn, though deep in her heart she knew she liked Jed best.

Giselle's father was an agent for a fishing co-op: her mother was a pharmacist. Her parents were strict churchgoers so Giselle had to go, too. She believed in God but wished worshipping Him wasn't so boring. The hour spent sitting still each Sunday was a torment to her.

For all her quickness of movement Giselle had a thoughtful face. Deep in her hazel eyes something sad and serious hid. Her hair, cut short, was brown, but in summer the same sun that tanned her skin bleached her hair, so that the darker became the lighter. It was astonishing that she stayed still long enough for the sun's rays to strike her but they somehow did find her and darken her.

What did Giselle think about behind those thoughtful, frightened eyes? She thought about her friends, Kate Nash, Sarah Scott, Nick Gibbons. She thought about how badly she wanted a horse, a dog, and a cat, in that order. She thought about becoming Prime Minister, about whether she was maybe adopted or not, about what would happen if she found out she had leukemia and the doctors gave her six months to live, about what would happen if her parents got killed in a car accident. She wondered when her breasts would grow, and how big they would be, and whether having her period would be good or bad. She dreamed about going on television and how proud everyone would be to know her.

When she crossed roads at intersections Giselle pretended that she was a horse in an important race, competing with the other pedestrians to be first to the other side. She usually won, except when she was with her parents or people she knew, and then she couldn't do it.

The deepest, biggest thought in Giselle, however, was something so bleak and frightening that she could never look at it. She knew it was there though, always there, like her dreams, like her doubts, like her lies. It occupied a large part of her. It was a sense of being incomplete, of there being something missing. It yawned inside her, gaping most hungrily when she was alone or tired or cold or scared, but always there.

Giselle didn't understand. She never understood, even when her mother one day at breakfast, talking about Giselle's ears, which stuck out, said, "But your brother's were the same." Her mother went red and quickly began clearing the table. Giselle went red and pretended she hadn't heard. Though she never understood, she carried a secret knowledge in her heart always. The knowledge fed on the hunger and the hunger fed on the knowledge.

THE ROAD was dusty and rutted. James walked cautiously along it. He didn't know very much about where he was. Bored and restless, fretting for some activity, he had punched a set of figures into the machine, noting anxiously as he did so that the needle on the battery indicator was starting to waver at around the halfway mark. He was sure only of the date—January 7, 1876—but was also fairly sure that he was somewhere in southern New South Wales.

As he rounded a long curve James heard the clatter of a horse's hooves in the distance. Hastily he jogged to a tree and slid behind it, as the noise grew louder. He peeped out when the rider went by, traveling at a quick clip. James had a glimpse of a young man, hatless, with a sunburned sweating face, mounted on a stringy tall mare. Heavy little clouds of dust followed him down the road.

James emerged again and continued walking. The bush was monotonous with scrub. The leaves hung listlessly in the heat. Peering carefully into the trees James saw, however, that there was activity in the shade, more than he had realized. Kangaroos seemed to be everywhere and birds were more numerous than he could remember ever having seen. A goanna started up out of the grass by the side of the road and strutted at speed across in front of the boy, who leaped backward, then ran back another twenty meters to be sure he was safe. When he continued on his way he did so even more warily.

A kilometer or so down the track James came unexpectedly to a white triangular stone marker sunk into the ground. It looked fresh and new. Painted on it in black was the letter G, with the numeral 6 underneath the letter. It was clearly a milestone, but James could not be sure what town it indicated. Goulburn? Gundagai? Grenfell?

But around the next bend was a scene that James recognized from television and old pictures. A prosperous-looking creek cut across the track: fat and healthy, it rolled and rattled away. Close to it a small fire poked its white streamer of smoke into the air. A few items of human property was scattered around: a blanket, some clothing, a couple of billies. Seeing nobody, James walked a few steps toward the fire, checking that the machine was in his hand and his finger close to the "Return" button. He stood and gazed, until a sudden rattling noise sent him into a spinning turn. The noise came from a man dragging firewood through the scrub. He was already within about twenty meters of James. Lean and dirty, followed by an equally lean and dirty yellow-brown dog, he seemed to take the boy's presence for granted. But the dog came sniffing around James, as though that were his right and his duty.

"G'day," the man said.

James gulped and nodded.

"You're young," the man said. "Where's your swag?"

James shrugged, then pointed down the track.

"What's the matter?" the man asked. "Cat got your tongue?"

James, deciding he would not talk, shrugged. The man grunted and pulled the branch he had carried closer to the fire. James noticed now how dirty everything was: the blanket, the billies, the fry pan. The dog finished examining the boy and trotted away about ten meters, squatting on the ground, as if to indicate his opinion of the visitor.

"Dressed kind of funny, aren't you?" the man asked, looking up from the fire. "Where'd you get that stuff? Where are you from?" James' grip tightened on the "Return" button but after waiting long moments for an answer the man seemed to give up. He turned away and picked up a billy.

"Want a cuppa?" he asked.

James nodded, and the swaggie went to the creek and filled the billy with water. He returned and settled the billy on the re-vitalized fire.

"Now," he said with satisfaction. "Time for a spot of lunch. Want a bite?"

James nodded again and the man cast around on the ground.

"Damn," he said. "Where's me bloody tucker box? Where'd I put it? Oh no!" he yelled suddenly, violently throwing his hat on the ground. "Oh, Jesus Christ, no!" He picked up a biggish stick and held it, clublike. James panicked and pressed the "Return" button. As he felt the disintegration begin he heard the swaggie's final shout. "The bloody dog's shat on me bloody tucker box."

"HAS ANYONE fed the dog?" their mother called, as she passed the door of the television room.

"I did it yesterday. It's James' turn," Ellie said, without taking her eyes from the screen.

"Yeah, after I'd done it every night for a week," James said.

"Oh! You liar!"

"I did. You never do it."

James rolled slowly off the bean bag and eased out of the room. He was sick of arguing and sick of Ellie. He went to the end of the yard and sat against the fence. It had been a hot slow day. Holidays were all right, he thought, but sometimes they got boring. He looked to his right and saw the crisscross of tracks in the dirt where he and Ellie had made a town and carved out roads. One of the cars they had been playing with was still there: a blue Volkswagen, peeping out from a minor cave-in at the end of a road.

A ladybird crawled past James. He picked it up and recited the traditional song:

> Ladybird, ladybird, fly away home.
> Your house is on fire and your children are gone,
> Except for the little one under the stone,
> Ladybird, ladybird, fly away home.

He blew on the ladybird but there was no response.

"Cruel mother," he muttered, repeating the verse and blowing harder. At last the insect spread its incongruous wings and flew from his hand: at first tentatively, then wheeling and soaring until it was gone. James was annoyed then that he had let it go.

Ellie came out of the house with the dog's bowl.

The dog bounced and bounced around her. She put it on the ground and the dog buried his nose in it, with eager woofling noises. Ellie came over to where James was sitting. She stood in front of him.

"You have to do it tomorrow night," she said.

James changed the subject.

"You know what the biggest difference is between animals and us?" he said.

"What?"

"We know we're going to die and they don't."

"But we don't really know we are. I mean, we pretend we're not."

"OK, what do you think the difference is, then?"

"I think the biggest difference is that we like beautiful things, just because they're beautiful. Animals don't understand beauty. Well, they don't seem to."

"They might, and we just don't realize it."

Ellie giggled.

"Can you imagine a cow looking at a painting and thinking how beautiful it is?"

He rolled over and picked up the toy Volkswagen.

"I'd hate to die in a car accident," he said. "I'd like to know beforehand, so you could go to Disneyland and everything. And so people could get you presents."

Ellie shivered.

"Gee, I don't want to know. I'd like it sudden. But not in a car crash. I hate the way Dad drives sometimes. He goes so fast. And through yellow lights."

"He's a good driver. I like going fast."

"I feel safer with Mum."

The dog, having emptied his bowl, came snuffling around James' feet, as though he might have food hidden in his socks.

"Go away," James said, grabbing him fiercely around his muzzle. The dog see-sawed his head to get free, planting his feet firmly on the ground and using the strength of his neck to buck the boy's hand off. James let his muzzle go, then got to his knees to wrestle in earnest as the dog obligingly returned to the fray. Ellie ran around them laughing. The dog bounded away then came circling back for more. Ellie grabbed his neck as James tried to roll him over, but he wriggled free and came leaping in on top of both of them. Ellie upended him and, as he lay on his back, they started roughing up his stomach. Then Ellie's wheezing excitement burst into asthma and she lost her noise and laughter and breath.

Later she said, "I hope I don't die of asthma."

Her comment made James nervous and embarrassed.

"Don't be stupid," he said.

"People do," she replied.

James didn't answer. He remembered the ladybird song.

THE HOSPITAL was a temporary one: a field hospital housed in an old convent. Its supplies were short and the girl did not appear to be badly hurt anyway. Her leg was broken in several places but it would heal. She had scratches, abrasions, bruises. She was in shock, malnourished, dehydrated. All of these things would heal, though they might leave scars. There were other patients more badly hurt; in some of them the candle flame of life was flickering, so that those watching over them hardly dared draw breath themselves, lest they take oxygen from the perilously light air flitting in and out of the tired lungs.

The scarring on the girl's face was old: it told nothing except that she had known pain before and had survived it.

Yet the expected healing did not seem to be taking place. The girl lay dry-eyed in her bed, complaining of nothing, accepting what was offered, but speaking to no one. She seemed to fade a little more every day, so that the early expectations of a quick discharge gave way to fears for her survival.

"If only she had her family . . . or a friend," a doctor said.

"Who knows we're here?" answered the nurse. "And we'll never have the time to go looking for her relatives. Maybe someone will turn up."

"Do you know where your parents are?" the doctor asked, leaning across the bed. There was no response. "I don't know if she understands a word I am saying," the doctor sighed, standing up again.

"I think she does," the nurse answered. "She seems to be listening to our conversation now."

The two women left the room, the nurse muttering to the doctor. "If she was with her family when the bomb went off I wouldn't hold much hope of her seeing them again."

Though she had spoken so quietly, the girl heard her.

WITH THE battery indicator now clearly on the wrong side of halfway, James knew that it was now or never for the next great experiment. He keyed in the latitude and longitude with little hesitation: 41° 0' 0", 75° 0' 0". But he trembled and sweated as he chose the date: 27. 09. 2099, 1000 hours. With a gulp, closing his eyes, he pressed "Enter."

His body seemed unaffected but something grew hot in his hands. With an effort he opened his heavy eyes and looked. Steam was coming out of the machine. It was heating up so quickly that already it was almost too hot to hold. James, desperate, stabbed at the "Return" button. He missed the first time, and now the machine felt like it was about to melt. James opened his hands to let it go. As it began to fall he stabbed at it a second time. Luckily he connected. The machine lay on the carpet and the steam began to clear.

Presently he was able to pick it up again without damage to his hands. Thoughtfully, he put it on his desk.

WAKING EARLY, in the luxury of the huge four-poster bed, Luke yawned and stretched and grinned. The old-fashioned starched white linen sheets felt purer and cleaner than anything he had experienced before. He wondered if it would be ridiculous to have fresh ironed sheets on the bed every night at home but realized reluctantly that neither he nor Sara would ever have time to do it. Most days they didn't even make the bed.

He turned on one side and looked out the windows to the long, sloping ornamental garden and the lawns and fountains beyond. Ever since he had been told about these stately homes his trips to Europe had been transformed. The same cool business transactions during the day but romance and majesty at night. The food and service often weren't too good but the surroundings made up for everything. And in this particular one, Castle Dundas, the surroundings were of a mediaeval perfection. The slight early morning haze combined with the ageless beauty of the gardens, so that Luke wondered lazily if he had slipped back into the fifteenth century.

He picked up his watch from the bedside table to look at the time, but the watch had stopped. He replaced it and yawned again. Then he turned on his side to face the door, as a gentle knock signaled a human arrival.

"Yes?" he called, before seeing that the door had already opened, and a young pageboy, quaintly dressed in an old-fashioned uniform, had come into the room.

"You have not put your boots out, sir," he said politely. Luke raised his eyebrows. This was another pleasant surprise, another reminder of the way things had once been.

"They're on the floor," he said, "in front of the television." The boy looked around him, but in a rather puzzled way, Luke watched him, equally puzzled.

"There," he said at last, pointing, "next to the red armchair." The boy, with a start, saw them and moved decorously to pick them up. Luke, in his lazily relaxed mood, decided to be friendly.

"What's your name?" he asked.

"Alexander," the boy replied. He still looked puzzled, but now his confusion seemed centered on the uncleaned shoes.

"How long have you been working here, Alexander?"

"Oh . . ." The boy's forehead puckered in thought. Luke decided that perhaps he was mentally disabled.

Finally Alexander answered, "Oh, a long time sir."

"And do you like it?"

"Oh . . . yes, sir." He looked suddenly nervous and covered his eyes with a hand. "I don't feel very well, sir," he mumbled.

"Well, leave the shoes," Luke urged. "Do you want me to call the manager?" But Alexander, ignoring him, was walking toward the door. Was it Luke's imagination, or did the boy seem to be growing smaller, to be shrinking within his clothes? Startled, Luke shook his head to clear the illusion, but by the time he had his clear sight back Alexander had gone out the door.

Luke lay and lazed for another hour or so. He had no early appointments and, though he did not know the time, he was sure it was still early. Finally, however, he got up, showered, dressed, and went downstairs for his breakfast. On the way to the dining room he passed the manager who gave him a smiling "good morning."

"Ah, good morning," Luke responded, stopping. "Look, I hope your bootboy's all right, is he? He seemed a bit off-color."

The manager suddenly looked remarkably alert.

"Sir?" he asked.

"The bootboy," Luke said again, ". . . er . . . Alexander."

The manager's face went white, then a slow gray.

"Sir," he said, "we have no bootboy."

Luke gaped and struggled for words. "No bootboy?" he said at last. "No bootboy?"

"No one, sir," said the manager and paused. "Sir," he said, "perhaps if you would eat now, I will try to explain to you after breakfast."

After the meal Luke eagerly sought out the manager, who, with a grave nod but no words, led Luke down a long corridor, and through a number of heavy doors. "We are in the private part of the castle," he explained to Luke. It was the first time he had spoken. Luke nodded a response.

They came to a small room fitted out as an office: it had a desk and two chairs, but these were dwarfed by the books, thousands of them, that filled every shelf and were piled in stacks on the floor. The manager sat Luke at the desk and indicated a row of books that were on the desk itself.

"These," he said, nodding, "are all about the castle." He picked out one, a thin, worn, green volume, and quickly found the page he wanted. "Sir," he said, placing it in front of the bemused man, "all of these books contain the story, if you wish to verify it. But this one tells it best, and it is in English." He bowed and began to leave. "You can find your way back?" he asked, from the doorway. "Yes," said Luke. The manager bowed again and left, shutting the door quietly behind him. Luke turned his attention to the book and began to read:

"Perhaps the saddest story associated with Castle Dundas is that of the little servant boy who has been said to haunt the west wing since 1832. Alexander Karatzann began work as a bootboy at the age of eleven. He was by all accounts a bright child who quickly became a favorite of the domestic staff. This makes his fate all the more tragic. On September 27, 1832, he was due to walk to his home, twelve miles away, for his weekly visit to his family. He did not return from this visit, and was presumed to be ill. Perhaps negligently, inquiries were not put into motion until September 29, when it was found that he had never reached his home. A search of the woods was instituted; several more days were wasted on this futile endeavor. It apparently did not occur to anyone that the boy might never have left the castle.

"No trace of the child was found.

"In 1864, an earth tremor caused the collapse of a large part of the derelict west wing. This event spurred the sixteenth Duke to take a step he had long contemplated: the rebuilding of the entire wing. The work commenced in 1865 with the hauling away of many tons of material from the sections affected by the earth tremor. As this rubble was being sorted—some for dumping in a nearby quarry, some for burning, and some for reuse—workmen came across an oak beam that had once straddled a door. On it was carved, in a childish hand, "Alexander Karatzann, September 28, 1832."

"There is still no explanation for the mystery. It was ascertained that workmen had been remodeling the west wing—which was still then in use—around the time that Alexander disappeared. Yet records and the memories of witnesses, though not entirely reliable, suggest that this work did not start until mid-October 1832. It is certain that the work included the sealing off of several apertures and sections of corridors, and two cellars that were considered unsafe. Though it was not possible to identify the room from which the oak beam had come, it was apparently not from a cellar.

"Continued searching found no other clues.

"The oak beam, with its pathetic inscription, has been kept by the family, along with an old leather purse with a crudely stitched 'A' on it. This, found jammed into a cracked flagstone that was replaced in 1925, is generally thought to have belonged to Alexander Karatzann.

"Continued interest in the story of this child has of course been due to the repeated and well-verified sightings of a ghost who resembles the boy in every material detail. Always seen in the west wing, and always in the month of September, the child is dressed in the livery of a nineteenth century servant. Many people claim to have held short conversations with him. They report that his initial lively demeanor soon gives way to a doleful and tragic expression, and the boy then fades away, literally in front of their eyes. Since the first sightings, in 1871, after the rebuilding of the west wing, a number of guests, frightened by these encounters, have left the castle vowing never to return. Others have not been so morbidly affected by the experience.

"Throughout the seventeenth century the main reception rooms of the castle were also supposed to be haunted, by the eighth Duchess, who committed suicide in 1601. However no sightings of this apparition have been reported since the early 1700s."

The book went on to discuss other tragedies associated with Castle Dundas, but Luke had read enough. He put the book down and sat staring straight ahead of him. There was consternation in his eyes, confusion and horror in his mind. How could something be real and not real? Be there and not there? People either lived or they didn't. How could somebody disappear as Alexander Karatzann had disappeared?

When Luke finally crept back down the long corridor he had no answers; indeed, an hour before he had hardly known that the questions existed.

JAMES HAD a whole day with Max and Sybil. They spent the morning at an aid organization for which the two teenagers did voluntary work, packing medical supplies for a field hospital. Sybil explained about the war, who was fighting and why. She showed him the main cities on a map and the places where the worst battles had been and the current location of the field hospital. She explained how a massive bomb, which exploded among fleeing civilians, had overloaded the hospital's facilities— hence the urgency of the need for equipment. James was fascinated. And he liked the neat arrangements of the supplies in their crates. He enjoyed helping. Later in the morning a young doctor who had been working in the hospital less than three days earlier came in to arrange consignment of the cases. They talked to her for a long time, too, and she described some of the patients and the difficulties of the work. James thought that he would like to be a doctor.

For lunch Sybil and Max and James went to an Italian restaurant which Max had heard was "great . . . the best." It was informal enough not to intimidate James, but the meal still did not go smoothly. As Sybil read the menu a corner of it got too close to the candle in the middle of the table and within a moment the menu had caught fire and was burning vigorously. Sybil threw her Coke over it to put it out, as the waiters came running. It was a long time before they were able to order from the now-charred menu. Then Max went to the toilet and came back with his fly undone. As he hastily did it up, with much embarrassment, he did not notice a waiter move the chair behind him to give himself a better route. Max sat down quickly, but kept going, straight to the floor. The whole restaurant was again disturbed. For the rest of the meal the waiter and even the customers gave their table a wide berth.

But even before that the service had been poor and the food was worse. They were all disappointed. They decided to cut the last course and the coffee, and get a Norgen-Vaas along the street. Sybil and Max went to the counter to pay the bill, James following them. He was startled to see Max, while the bill was being rung up on the cash register, pick up a couple of pieces of garlic bread from a basket on the nearest table, and, after easing up the cover on the Espresso machine, drop the bread into the bubbling coffee. James opened his mouth as if to say something. But Max caught his eye and winked. James shut his mouth again.

When they were back on the street again Max gave an exultant whoop. "Fixed their coffee for them," he laughed, dancing along the street, in an excess of delight.

THIS HOUSE is full of quiet cold air. My room's the only place where it doesn't spread, although sometimes people open the door and let in the draft. It smells minty. They don't open it easily or comfortably, for the door is shut with my mind and my will as well as with its own metal grip. I hear them slowly disturbing the air in other parts of the house, too, with flat deliberate movements, a walk of footsteps, the "aarrchhh" of a chair being pushed back, the commotion of plates and cups.

I keep my room warm with my books, with my clothes thrown across the floor and stuffed into drawers, with my drawings and posters stuck on the walls, with my smelly old sneakers wrestling with each other in a corner, with my tree at the window. I keep it warm by sitting at my desk and thinking and writing.

The heart of the room is the bottom drawer of my desk. In there sits an envelope. It's so warm I can't pick it up but sometimes I open the drawer and peer in to make sure it's still there. It always has been so far. In that envelope are all the little bits of her, like the fragments after an explosion. There are only two photos (all the ones in the house were gone). One of them I cut out of the school magazine in the library. It's just the ordinary old class photo. She's in the back row, third from the left. The other one is from a time capsule we buried in our cubby when we were little. And there are three birthday cards she gave me; and the lucky dollar that she lent me for the slalom championships, that I forgot to give back; and her silver chain with a cross that I found behind the washing machine a long time later; and her little Teddy Bear—the size of a bottle of Liquid

Paper—that a friend of hers, Van, slipped into my pocket at school one day, without saying anything; and a note she wrote me, nothing important, just saying she'd taken back the videos; and her broken pencil sharpener; and half her book mark and her tooth that I'd replaced with two dollars when I was baby-sitting one night. I think that's all. I know that's all.

Sometimes I think if you understand things then you can fix them.

Maybe in this cold quiet house there are other little warm spots, glowing with secret life. Where are they? If I look, will I find them? They used to be so obvious: the biscuit jar, the television, the fireplace, our cubby, her bedroom, the old chair with its worn arms where our other grandmother used to sit. Maybe the other people who live here have their own ones. I suppose they must.

And what about me? Me, the person me, I mean. My cold quiet body, I mean. When I'm in my room I feel that little parts of me might be alive—my mouth, my heart, my hands. When I'm in my own room, yes, I feel something.

My favorite poem is so light in words, so heavy in everything else:

> I never parked in my own driveway
> In case you wanted to leave.
> And sooner or later you all did.
> I waved you down the path
> Then turned
> And went back inside the house.

I used to keep it on the wall but now it's on the desk, under some books.

There's movement downstairs again: footsteps echoing like a pulse. The third step from the bottom of the staircase sends a quiver along the upstairs corridor when anyone treads on it. The building trembles.

THEY WERE on holiday when Ellie had a series of asthma attacks so bad that she was admitted to hospital. The attacks continued and she had to stay there for some weeks. For James the days passed with little distinction between them. The holiday turned into a long one; they were forced to keep extending their booking at the big resort hotel.

They were staying near the sea. Only a golf course lay between the hotel and the barren rocky coastline. Inland was all farming country, soft green that rolled on and on for many miles. The soil was rich; a dark brown that looked good enough to eat.

James roamed the hills freely. He became a little wild. His parents preferred the attractions inside the hotel: the bar, the casino, the swimming pool. They went to the hospital to visit Ellie. James did not know how often. He himself went every couple of days. He did not mind going, but he had to be sought, through the paddocks, on the distant hills, and called and called, reeled in on an invisible line of obedience and family. The line was a long one and it had its weak points, where James stopped to examine a tree trunk or a hole in the ground. It never brought him in directly but always in wide, far-reaching zigzags, like a salmon fighting an angler.

After he'd visited the hospital a few times he started to notice the boy in the bed next to his sister. Thin and pale, the boy never seemed to have visitors. James approached him with extreme diffidence but was surprised and relieved by the boy's eager welcome. Each time he visited Ellie he made a point of spending some time with the little boy, more and more on each visit, until he was splitting the visiting hours equally between the two.

Ellie looked terrible, using an oxygen mask frequently, struggling to breathe, struggling to speak. James hated seeing her like that. He didn't understand asthma: it was a disease that defied his imagination. He could imagine what it would feel like to have a broken leg; he understood the logic of cancer and heart attacks; he had himself struggled through childhood bouts of scarlet fever, mumps, and measles. But asthma was an enigma, a frustrating and elusive illness that made him angry and upset.

One day, in a paddock behind a line of trees, out of sight of the nearest farmhouse, James cornered a small pocket of sheep. Although one after another slipped under his guard and accelerated along the fenceline James gradually closed in until he could grab one of the startled, heaving beasts by the fleece. When this sheep bolted, too, James used its momentum to swing himself onto its back and ride it for a few breathtaking, jolting meters. The sheep, however, showed surprising intelligence. Or perhaps it was lucky, and its instincts coincided with its interests. Whichever, it suddenly swerved, continuing to gallop parallel to the fence, but now so close that the barbed wire dragged along James' flank, tearing at his clothes and his skin. Suddenly the ride became a panic-stricken struggle by James to get off. It took him so long that he felt he would never succeed. His dismounting was half a tumbling twist by him, half a bucking twist by the sheep as it ran. He landed on his shoulder, then rolled over and over in the dirt, panting and crying. "Damn sheep," he swore futilely, angrily. "Fat, stupid, bloody, ugly, dumb bastard. I hate it, I hate it." He could not understand how something apparently so benign could so thoroughly overthrow him.

He told no one about the sheep except the little boy in the hospital. The boy laughed and laughed. As James was leaving the ward the charge sister said to him, "My word, you've done Alex good with your visits. He's been a different boy since you took an interest in him."

James felt confused, but proud and delighted. A few days later Ellie was discharged and they were able to begin the long journey home. James never saw Alex again but he often wondered about him, hoping the child had recovered from his illness and been allowed home.

THE GIRL lay listlessly in her hospital bed. Somebody, in an effort to cheer her, had cut out various articles from an old Australian magazine and pinned them on the wall. The girl practiced her English by reading them over and over. The one she read most often showed a photograph of an ancient, incredibly lined black face, with eyes that seemed to gaze through and beyond the camera and the viewer and even time itself. Its headline read: "Language Passes with Moonlight." It told how an Aboriginal woman called Lardie Moonlight had just died in the state of Queensland. She had been the last person to speak an Aboriginal language called Kalkadoon and with her death the language had gone forever. It had been a complex and sophisticated language and, although its basic elements had been recorded by linguists, its subtleties were lost—and it would never be used in speech again.

The article went on to say that what had happened to Kalkadoon was common. In Australia alone hundreds of languages had disappeared.

There were eight articles stuck on the wall, although two soon fell off and wafted under the bed where they lay gathering dust. Of the ones that remained, most were light and bright. In fact the space seemed to be taken up mainly by advertisements: Coca Cola, Seppelt's Wines, Target Stores. But it was the article about Lardie Moonlight that fascinated the girl. It made her feel empty and awful and hopeless, yet she kept rereading it.

One day her tired eyes were resting on an advertisement for a range of watches called Wardill. On the golden-brown skin of a model's arm gleamed a golden watch. The caption read, "For people who don't always care what time it is." The girl amused herself by straining to read the time on the watch in the photo but she was a little too far away. She could not be sure if she was seeing the hands of the watch or just imagining lines on the paper. The effort made her eyes hurt and she screwed them shut for a long moment, then opened them again. To her astonishment a boy was now standing between her and the magazine pictures on the wall. She had not heard him come in and she could not imagine how he had come there so quickly. He was of Caucasian appearance, about twelve years old perhaps, with light brown hair and darker brown eyes. He was watching her tensely, unblinking. The girl gulped and swallowed. Suddenly she was tired of not speaking. She said in her own language, "Where did you come from?"

He came a step closer to the bed but he showed no understanding of her question. She repeated it in English. This time he answered.

"Oh . . . um . . . out there." He waved vaguely toward the door. His voice was very husky and faint. Then he asked, "You've broken your leg?"

"Yes," she said. "There was . . . a big bang. Everything fell over. It was a bomb, I suppose." Suddenly she was very tired. She closed her eyes for a minute. When she opened them again she expected to find him gone. But he was still there.

"Where are your family?" he asked.

"I don't know," she said. She began to cry. "They were in front of me. I stopped . . . then everything fell down. I don't know where they are. I think they're dead. In the ground and dead."

"When did it happen?" he asked. His voice was gaining strength and sounded urgent.

"I don't know," she said. "Maybe a week. Maybe two. I was under the wall . . . for a long time."

Frustrated, the boy looked around the room, searching for clues. There was a collection of scraps of paper tied to the wall with a string which hung from a nail. He detached them and looked at them. They were in a language he did not know. He brought them to her.

"What are these?" he asked. She peered at them.

"That's my name," she said, pointing to some words at the top of the first page. She read on, translating, in a faltering voice.

"It says I am found buried," she said, "about a kilometer from here in the Freedom Square . . . I am . . . I'm not sure how you say . . . asleep?"

"Unconscious," he prompted.

"I have the broken leg. And other things. Cuts. And bangs on my head."

"When was this?" he interrupted.

"July 8," she read.

"What time?"

"Half past three in the afternoon . . ." She read on. "But . . . I am in the ground . . . maybe three days. It says "Bury by bomb explosion since 11 A.M., July 4."

"11 A.M.," he repeated. "July 4."

She put the notes down and lay back on the bed. "Who are you?" she asked again. "Why do you want to know? Are you sick, too? Do you work here?"

"I'm a visitor," he said. "Just a visitor."

She was puzzled by this.

"Where do you live? Where are your family?"

"A long way away." He grinned shyly. "A long way away."

"If you want to help me," she said, and her eyes filled with tears again. "Find my parents . . . in this Freedom Square."

"How will I know them?" he asked.

She frowned with the effort of remembering, and spoke slowly: "My mother wears a blue and white scarf. Dark blue and white. She is small and old. She has a mark on the back of her neck . . . like this." She touched her face, paused a moment, then kept talking. "My father is taller. His teeth are not very good. The front one is chipped. He wear glasses. He has no hair on the top of his head. His eyebrows, they come together, nearly, in the middle."

Her voice had been fading for the last few minutes. Now she closed her eyes. Her breathing gradually became even and audible. James waited for a few minutes to see if she would wake up.

When she didn't he reached into his pocket and took out Mr. Woodforde's machine.

WITH FEAR flapping and squeezing inside his chest James moved slowly through the square, searching the faces of the people. His hands were sweaty but soon he was sweating everywhere. Many people glanced quickly and curiously at him, for he did not look like any of the others who were using the square as a thoroughfare. But they were too intent on their own interests to give him any lingering attention. He was free, as free as the traffic and his fear would allow, to conduct his search.

Knowing that the timing given on the sheet was likely to be an approximation, he had set his arrival for ten fifteen. It was obvious that the square was whole then, teeming with uninterrupted life. He edged backward and forward through the people, scanning the faces, aware of the price of failure. His hand was on the "Return" button, always, but he also knew that if he was at the wrong spot at the wrong time his reflexes might not be quick enough.

At about ten to eleven a new wave of people came through the square. James saw a group of nuns, their habits dusty at their ankles, moving through the crowd like beetles in a drought. He was alarmed to see a soldier approaching him with a purposeful look in his eyes. The boy began sidling away. As he did so he thought he glimpsed the girl, about forty or fifty meters away. He turned and plunged toward the spot, intent upon getting there before looking for her again. He knew that if it were she, he might have only seconds to make the vital contact. He wriggled and worried his way through the cumbersome, overloaded people. But when he had traveled about thirty meters he nearly ran into her. He pulled up with a little cry of surprise. She glanced at him without expression, then looked again, this time with puzzled eyes. "Was that a glance of recognition?" he wondered, feeling somehow, illogically, guilty as he slipped around behind her. She was wearing a gray cotton shift over gray cotton trousers and carrying an assortment of heavy bags. Her long black hair ran straight and pleasingly down her back. She stopped and changed several of the bags around, to alter the balance of the load. As she did so, two people in front of her turned. The man was tall, with thinning black hair and dark eyebrows that nearly met in the middle. He was wearing glasses. The woman was smaller and looked older. She had a blue and white scarf around her neck. She smiled at the girl. Then the two adults turned back and continued to forge their way through the throng.

James, now in a panic, darted off in a wide circle that brought him out well in front of them. He turned and stood on his toes, searching to identify them again. He saw that the girl had stopped a second time to adjust her load. Her parents, unnoticing, had continued on their way and a gap had been created between them and their daughter. James opened his mouth to shout a warning. But his voice was lost in a great thunder of sound that suddenly rolled up all around him. The ground was lifted from under his feet and he with it. Although he was raised only about a meter, it seemed to take forever before he was dropped again. When he was dropped it was as though the ground had been assembled and aligned in a new way and would never be the same again.

The roar of noise was continuing undiminished when a wall

fell just meters from the boy, and he saw people disappear under the cruel cutting stone. Others ran past him, mouths silently open, eyes staring. Everything seemed to be falling, and he was appalled at how long it took. He had shocking, intimate, sudden views of what people looked like inside when they were cut open. He saw people pinned down in an instant, so that they were writhing and flapping like fish in the bottom of a boat. He saw moments of nobility, as people ran back to help others who had fallen, or used their bodies to shield their children. And he saw moments of madness, as people rushed straight under collapsing walls and a man ran back into danger to pick up a small saucepan that his son had dropped.

As the noise at last began to slow and lessen, he saw the girl's parents. They seemed to be unharmed, standing in a clear part of the square, looking frantically around them. Dust and smoke and unnatural breezes were making it difficult to see, but it was obvious that the girl, their daughter, was nowhere to be seen. They talked madly to each other, arms pointing to where they thought she might have been and might now be. Then they began tearing at the rubble with their bare hands. James ran over and helped them, despite his certain knowledge that it was useless. They paused to gaze blankly at him for a moment, then the man said something before they resumed ripping at the rocks and mortar.

Gradually, as the square settled into its new composition of sight and sound, the first frenzy was replaced by a steady, sweating digging. In various parts of the ruins others were digging, too. After some time they exposed the body of a baby, terribly dead. James did not know whether to look at it or not but he helped lay it out under a little shelter of masonite. He recognized and trembled at the memories that this invoked in him. Then he returned to the pitiful scrape they had made in the rubble.

After half an hour or so the conditions in the square changed again. Soldiers began to arrive, some in trucks, some on foot. A few ambulances came in a hurry, and were surrounded. The soldiers took charge. They had some shovels and picks and, as the morning became afternoon, more and more tools appeared. By about four o'clock the scene was one of methodical, if slow, activity. At that point the remaining civilians, James among them, were pushed away from the diggings, until they were massed in a corner of the square, under the supervision of two soldiers. Though many protested at this treatment their protests were ignored. James, whose presence was starting to attract curious glances again, went willingly enough with them. He knew he had to. But he kept his hand on Mr. Woodforde's machine, which was thrust deep in his pocket.

Little happened for a while. The soldiers kept working. From time to time there was a flurry of movement as bodies, some dead, some alive, were discovered and lifted carefully from the ruins. At these moments the civilians who were with James crowded as close as they were allowed, to see if they could identify their relatives. They shouted questions at the soldiers but they were ignored, and the bodies taken away in trucks and ambulances.

Later in the afternoon a bus arrived and the civilians, despite tears and protests and struggles, were loaded into it. The soldier in charge of this operation pulled James aside and talked at him in a rattle of words that James was not able to understand. But finally, seeing the boy's lack of comprehension, he pushed him on board with the others. In a cloud of smoke from the exhaust and amid wails from its passengers, the vehicle began its journey.

The bus was crowded but the journey was mercifully short. After a little time they passed the old convent which James recognized as the building which would soon house the girl with the scarred face. About fifty kilometers further on, along a route which James strove carefully to memorize, they were disembarked at a place that defied definition. It was a collection of huts and tents, side by side with what appeared to be a large rubbish tip. It was surrounded by various types of wire, some lengths of which were placarded with red crosses. The whole place was guarded, but in a fairly casual way. In one corner was a group of old tanks, with mechanics working on them. In a central square about a hundred people were gathered, listening to a speech by a woman in uniform who stood precariously on a black plastic barrel. The bus passengers were ushered to a shambles of galvanized iron shelters and it was made apparent to them that this would be their accommodation.

Deciding that his position might soon become precarious, James waited long enough to watch the girl's parents settle themselves into an iron lean-to. Then he slipped behind a wall and used his "Return" button.

HE TRIED to get back into the house without being seen. It should have been easy, as it was nearly dark. But to his surprise there were people all around the building. As he turned a corner he found himself a meter away from his mother. She was facing in his direction and saw him instantly.

"James!" she cried. "Where have you been? I can't believe it! We've been looking everywhere! We've got the Police here and Security and everything! Oh, where have you been?" James stood staring silently at her. He noted with some surprise that there were tears in her eyes. She leaned against the wall and her shoulders convulsed as she half-covered her face with her hands. James' father came across the garden, through the trees. When he saw James he started to hurry. James darted past, to the verandah, and entered the house. As he did so he heard his father reach his mother and his mother say, "Oh God, what are we going to do? I think he's getting worse." His father answered in a low tone. James could not hear the actual words. He ran upstairs to his bedroom.

HE SAT at the window of his bedroom as the darkness brushed past. The night air whistled and whispered its many possibilities. James put out a hand and twisted a leaf around his fingers. He peered across at the old Lab 17, hoping against hope that a light would be showing in it, like old times. But the building was so dark that he had trouble making it out. He sighed and looked away, up at the sky. A few stars showed through the branches and leaves of the tree, but most were obscured. The flashing light of a satellite appeared on its steady journey across the heavens. James followed it with unwavering concentration until it was out of sight. Then, when it was gone, he sighed again, pushed himself up out of his seat by his hands and went to bed. He lay awake, his mind in turmoil. The thoughts crowded around, jumping the queue, piggybacking on each other, leading him in and out of mazes and through mirrors. After a while, still unable to sleep, he turned the bed lamp on and picked up the book he was reading. It was called *Case in Court*. An old book, by a man he had never heard of. He read again a section he had first come across a few weeks earlier:

At about two A.M. on the morning of the 6th November, 1939, a motor car burst into flames some 200 yards from the village of Hardingstone, near Northampton. It was first noticed by two young men returning home from a dance, who saw a bright light further down the road. At the same time a man came out of a ditch by the side of the road and walked past them without speaking. Just after he passed them, he looked back and said, "It looks as if somebody has had a bonfire." He then walked on down the road, seeming to hesitate as to which way to go, then turned toward London and disappeared. That man was Rouse. He was subsequently identified by the two young men and his identity must be taken as sufficiently established without the necessity for any admission of his own. The two men ran toward the flames and then saw that it was a motor car blazing furiously by the side of the road. They ran on to the village and came back with the village constable. They were unable to approach the blazing car until the flames died down. They then discovered something inside which turned out to be the body of a dead man. They could make no further investigation until the fire was extinguished, by which time the car was completely demolished. It is not perhaps surprising that the trial of Rouse for the murder of the man found inside the car was described as a mystery, because from that day to this no one has ever known who the dead man was, or how or for what purpose he was killed.

The action of the police on discovering the body was not particularly helpful to themselves. No photographs were taken of the body or of the car before it was moved, and the car itself was left unwatched by the police for a considerable period.

James laid down the book, turned out the light again and went back to the window. A baby possum that the boy had been feeding occasionally ran along a branch near the window. He was growing big and fat. But a clanging noise from a nearby building frightened him and he hurried further up the tree, with a clatter of leaves and twigs. James noticed that, unlike past days, the possum did not scuttle to his mother when alarmed. James was pleased in a way by the increased independence and maturity of the little creature but disappointed, too, as the baby possums were always more tractable and trusting. Seeing the mother on a branch just below him James called out quietly but firmly to her, "Yes, Ma P, you're going to have to let him go. He's too big for you now. He won't be coming by so often."

Suddenly he realized with a shock that he was hearing his own voice inside his own house. He withdrew his head quickly and hoped that no one had been listening.

THERE WERE only two things that he could imagine might be wrong. One was that the parents might have moved, or been moved, from the camp, and he would not be able to find them. The second was that he might not be able to convince them to come with him. He could think of other problems, too, but none that should be beyond his competence.

The first problem turned out not to be one at all, though he got the impression that he was just in time. He found the parents sitting at one end of the biggest compound, with their pitiful bags of possessions at their feet. They had the appearance of people about to resume a journey. Rather to his surprise they recognized him and showed pleasure at the sight of him. They evidently remembered him as a digging partner in the excavations back in Freedom Square. They may not have realized that they were digging for the same girl—though James, knowing what he did, had dug with little zeal—but perhaps they sensed that their purpose had been the same.

They were puzzled but willing when James beckoned them away. And they brought their possessions with them when he indicated that they should. They followed him to one of the rough wire fences that formed a boundary of the camp. James had timed his arrival for dusk but the security around the area was now so lax that they could probably have slipped away in daylight. James gestured to the man and the woman that they should follow him across the crude barrier. But this was not so easily managed. The old people showed reluctance, concern. They looked at him questioningly, hands outstretched, palms upward. James had thought of only one solution to this predictable dilemma and he was not sure that it was going to be good enough to work. He took a stick and began drawing in the dust. First he drew an irregular figure in the approximate shape of the camp. Then he drew a winding road, pointing away to the north as he did so. Finally he drew a building with a large cross on it. He looked up. The two parents were watching him carefully. He reached across to the face of the mother and gently drew on it with his thumb the exact shape of their daughter's scar. At last he had broken through their reserve. They talked to each other excitedly. He could not tell what their decision was likely to be, though he scanned their faces anxiously and tried to pick up the nuances in their conversation. They talked for several minutes. Though James could not know it, they were agreeing that this strange Caucasian boy seemed to be offering them their only chance to find their daughter. No matter what the dangers of going with him, they could not afford not to go. And why should he wish them any harm anyway? Surely one so young would not go to all this trouble out of malice?

And so at last they turned and looked at James gravely, nodded their heads and gestured to him to lead them. It was now quite dark. It was not clear what would happen to anyone who tried to leave the camp—perhaps nothing—but the three of them exercised great care when getting across the fence. Within ten minutes however they were on a dirt track, hurrying away from the enclosed area. And soon they were on the road that James recognized, the road they had been taken down on their journey from Freedom Square, the road north. Within another ten minutes, James, knowing that they could not walk the entire way and knowing that his time was limited, began trying to thumb a lift. After a short time they were picked up by an army truck.

IN HER dreary hospital bed the girl shifted restlessly for a moment, before lying back on the pillow and slipping again into the pallid, vapid state that was causing her doctor more concern each day. Her eyes settled on a dead spider that hung in its own web in a corner of the ceiling. The spider, lifeless, moved and lifted at the merest breath of a breeze. The girl felt that if she blinked the spider would dance. She tried it. To her astonishment the spider bounced and spun. Then she realized that its activity was precipitated not by the flick of her eyelids but by the door to her small room, which had opened quietly. She turned her head slowly, listlessly, and saw a sight she had believed she would never see again. One parent would have made her happy. Two were overwhelming. The shock and joy of the reunion was so violent that afterward none of the three could remember anything of it. They came gradually to the realization that they were together, gathered in and around a bed in a makeshift hospital. By the time they thought to look for James again, he was gone.

AFTER JAMES' last use of Mr. Woodforde's machine he could not quite remember whether he had actually used it or whether he had merely used his memory and his mind. It was his last night with Ellie. She had asthma all day, and his parents had left her at home with him, telling him to "look after her, be careful with her." His parents had gone to a birthday party for one of the researchers at a restaurant. It wasn't even someone they liked, but it was a party. James was annoyed at them for going, sulky when they actually left. He ignored Ellie for the first half-hour or so, refusing to take his eyes from the TV when she spoke, trying to shut out the noise of her ragged, hungry breathing.

"What do you want to eat?" he at last asked ungraciously, getting up and taking a couple of steps toward the kitchen.

"Nothing," she said.

"Don't be stupid, you've got to eat something."

"Why?"

"Cos you'll starve if you don't."

"I don't want anything."

"Well, this is your only chance. I'm going to make myself some tea now, and I'm not making anything later just for you."

"OK, don't." Then she added, as he went to the door, "What are you having?"

"I don't know, I'll see what's there. Probably microwave something. Are there any of those hamburgers left?"

"Don't think so, unless Mum got some more. I had the last one yesterday."

She drew back, into and under her doona, as James went out to the kitchen. "Stupid asthma," he thought, "I hate it. Half the time she puts it on, anyway."

At about eight o'clock they had a foul argument over television shows. Ellie wanted to watch "Do We Dare?"; James wanted to watch "Highway 32."

Ellie was in tears. James was being cold and sarcastic.

"Go and watch it upstairs if you want to see it that badly," he said at last.

"No, you go, why should I go?"

"'Do We Dare' is so dumb. Guess it's lucky 'Sesame Street' isn't on or you'd want to watch that."

James prevailed, largely because he had the remote control. Ellie stayed huddled in her doona, sucking her thumb, only half-watching the television. Wet tear traces, like snail tracks, marked each cheek. Occasionally she gave a little sob. Her breathing was worse.

"Do you want the pump?" he said at last.

"Yes, please."

"Can you wait until the next ad?"

"OK."

A few minutes later James switched channels to "Do We Dare?." "'Highway 32' is pathetic now, since Johnno left," he said. He was rewarded by a tiny flash of a smile from Ellie through the mask.

She went to bed at about nine, saying she felt better, although she did not look it.

"Do you want me to carry you up?" he asked, not sure that he could anyway.

"Nuh," she said, "I'm too fat and heavy for you."

"You're not fat," he said.

Later, when he went to bed himself, he noticed that her light was still on. He hesitated by her door, wondering if he should disturb her or not. She was such a light sleeper. He went on to his own room. He awoke only once during the night, when his parents came home. They sounded drunk, laughing and crashing around. He wrinkled his face in disgust, rolled over and went to sleep.

In the morning James came down to breakfast very late. It was the third day of the school holidays. His grandmother was there. No one else seemed to be around.

"Hurry up," she said. "I've been waiting for you. You're coming to stay with us. Get a few things from your room, and I'll wait for you in the car."

There was nothing unusual in this, as he always stayed with them for part of the holidays, and often at short notice. He did as she directed. But he soon realized that this time it was different. No one seemed to want to speak to him. He stayed there a few days, a week, a fortnight. Then, just before it was time to go back to school, his grandmother told him that Ellie had died "two weeks ago, the night you were supposed to look after her." On the day that school started he found his uniform had mysteriously appeared and was hung on the chair in the room he was staying in. He put it on and was driven to school. This became routine. The weeks became months, and still he was staying at his grandparents'. And still they hardly spoke to him. He had not seen his parents since the night they went to the party, though day and night he longed for them, with an awful deep longing. He longed for their touch. But he dared not ask anyone about them. The kids and teachers at school seemed to be colder, too, to be withdrawing. Then James became ill. He had acute peritonitis. He lay in a hospital bed, hoping he would die. One day, after the crisis had passed, he opened his eyes and saw what he had been praying for months to see. His parents were standing by the side of the bed. He closed his eyes and turned away from them. They made many efforts to get him to turn back again, to open his eyes, to speak to them. After a while they gave up and went away. When he was discharged from hospital it was to his parents' place that he was taken, but he did not speak to them or to anybody.

Time passed.

JAMES PRESSED the "Return" button. Or did he? Had he really been there with Ellie again? Had he really heard her wheezing giggle when she told him she was too fat? Had he only imagined her darting grateful smile when he told her she wasn't? Had he imagined standing at her door, the door that he had been afraid to open ever since that night and was still afraid to open? Was it terrible, the knowledge behind that door?

HIS PARENTS were sitting at the kitchen table, talking in low voices, when James walked in. They ceased their conversation and looked at him in some surprise, coffee mugs halfway to their mouths. James said, clearly and calmly, "Do you think it's my fault Ellie died?" There was a long silence. James did not drop his eyes. At last his father put down his coffee mug on the table with a little clicking noise. There was another pause. Then he said slowly and carefully, "No . . . No . . . I don't think that. We never thought that. We just messed it all up. We were so mad with it all, I guess we messed everything up." His mother said, "We couldn't think straight. By the time we started to function again, the damage was done."

James sat down on the chair at the end of the table.

JAMES TURNED the machine on and began keying in the new coordinates. But the machine felt cold and dead. He glanced at the battery indicator and saw with shock that the needle had hardly moved. He flicked the switch on and off several times. Each time the needle gave only a tremble. The last time it seemed not to move at all.

He pried open the cover of the little battery compartment and pulled out the battery. Bright, bright silver, it was like no other power source he had ever seen. It was tiny; the size of a gambling die. And the shape of one. But it was surprisingly heavy, weighing more than all the rest of the machine. James sat and stared at it for several minutes, as it rested in the palm of his hand. Then he made his decision. He ran downstairs, through the front door and across the square to the Technicians' Store. A tall young man, fair-haired, with a drooping mustache, was standing behind the counter. An array of parts was spread in front of him. James had seen the young man many times. He deposited the tiny battery on the counter.

The man looked at it casually, looked at James, looked at it again, then picked it up. Suddenly his whole expression changed. He was astonished. He seemed almost frightened. He stared at James. "Where did you get this?" he said. "Where'd you get this? This isn't possible. How could you have one of these?" He turned it over and over, shaking his head. "Someone said the other night that you probably see more of what goes on around here than anyone. I'm starting to believe it." He bent toward James. "Where did you get it? Why did you bring it to me?"

"I want you to recharge it," James said. His voice sounded perfectly normal, steady and well-modulated. The man showed astonishment a second time.

"I'll be," he muttered. "Talkative little fellow aren't you? Look," he said, "you don't recharge them. They're not like a battery. But on the other hand, you can't run them out either. Well, not that anyone's been able to so far. If you've been running your torch off it, then I guarantee you a few millenia of bright light yet. Matter of fact, you could keep this base lit up for way past your lifetime, just on one of these little beauties."

"It's finished," James said.

The man looked away, around the store, shaking his head. "I don't think I want to know about this," he muttered. "Not in my last week. What do you mean 'It's finished?'" He waited but James did not answer. "Look," he said at last, "I'll check it anyway . . . That can't do any harm." He took it to a large tank-like container at the side of the room, undid three heavy latches, placed it inside, and sealed the tank again. He used a wheel to spin it shut. Various whirring noises were emitted by the machinery. The man stood there looking at a panel of gauges and dials. "You're right," he said at last, flatly. He unsealed the tank and brought the little cube back to James, placing it on the counter between them. "It's impossible but you're right."

"I think I've got this figured out," he said quietly. "Mr. Woodforde. You used to hang round there a lot. That old bugger must have actually brought it to the production stage. God knows where or how. It couldn't have been in that lab. The old devil. He was always telling me he was going to win a Nobel Prize." He laughed. James was transfixed. "I'm not sure how much I want to know," the man continued. "I'm leaving next week. Me and my girlfriend are sailing away in our boat. Around the islands." He paused again, then drew breath and asked the critical question.

"Who used up all the energy in this thing?" he asked. "You or Mr. Woodforde? And what on?"

The boy took refuge in the time-honored line of all children, and many adults.

"I don't know," he said.

The man sighed. "I don't know whether to be relieved or disappointed," he confessed. "Relieved, I think." He shrugged.

"Well, what are we going to do with it? Do you want me to get rid of it? If they know you've got one they'll never leave you alone. They'll pressure you till you're coming apart at the seams. And if they think I even know these little varmints exist they'll never let me leave. I know you can keep a secret. And I know I can. And I also know how to dispose of it safely. Wanna leave it with me?"

"OK," James said equably. He started toward the door.

"Been nice talking to you," the man said softly. "Been . . . nice talking to you.